RUTH AI

A HOUSE IN THI

RUTH AUGUSTA ADAM (1907-1977) was born Ruth King in Nottinghamshire. In early adult life she taught for five years in poverty-stricken Nottinghamshire elementary schools. In 1932 she married Kenneth Adam, a journalist on the *Manchester Guardian* who later became the first director of BBC television.

Between 1937 and 1947 Ruth Adam had four children and worked for the Ministry of Information during the war. She wrote several novels of social reportage, as well as non-fiction titles, radio scripts, and journalism: the latter in part a platform for her Christian socialist feminist views.

In 1955 Ruth Adam, with her friend Peggy Jay, co-founded the Fisher Group, a think-tank on social policy and family matters. Arising out of this concern she wrote her novels *Fetch Her Away* (1954) and *Look Who's Talking* (1960) about girls in care. In contrast is her novel *A House in the Country* (1957), a comic account of her family's attempt at living in a commune. At the end of her life came *A Woman's Place, 1910–1975*, a succinct, witty, and trenchant social history of British women in the twentieth century.

Ruth Adam died at the Hospital of St John and St Elizabeth, Marylebone, London, in 1977.

TITLES BY RUTH ADAM

Fiction for Adults

War on Saturday Week (1937)
I'm Not Complaining (1938)
There Needs No Ghost (1939)
Murder in the Home Guard (1942)
Set to Partners (1947)
So Sweet a Changeling (1954)
Fetch Her Away (1954)
A House in the Country (1957)
Look Who's Talking (1960)

Fiction for Children

A Stepmother for Susan of St. Bride's (1958)
Susan and the Wrong Baby (1961)

Non-Fiction

They Built a Nation: A Child's History of America (1963)
Beatrice Webb: A Life, 1858-1943 (1967)
A Woman's Place 1910-1975 (1975)

RUTH ADAM

A HOUSE IN THE COUNTRY

With an introduction by

Yvonne Roberts

DEAN STREET PRESS

A Furrowed Middlebrow Book
FM48

Published by Dean Street Press 2020

First published in 1957 by Frederick Muller

Cover by DSP

ISBN 978 1 913527 23 5

www.deanstreetpress.co.uk

INTRODUCTION

IN TIMES of crisis, dreams flourish to keep the spirits fired. So, during the years of World War II. In *A House in the Country*, four men and two women, tired of blackouts, powdered eggs and cramped air raid shelters, fantasise about moving out of London to a baronial manor house "with acres and acres of gardens" and its own river. "This is a cautionary tale and true," writes Ruth Adam who based the novel, published in 1957, on her own post-war experience of living communally with several other families. "Never fall in love with a house."

Together, Ruth and her glamorous co-residents including her unnamed husband, (Kenneth Adam who later became Director of the B.B.C.), their three children, Ruth's brother, Bob, in the R.A.F., Diana, a West End actress, Lefty in the navy and Timmy, a "golden-voiced" broadcaster, conjure a rural refuge with "red-flagged floors and hams hanging in the kitchen" where they will be serenaded by bird song not air raid sirens and enjoy nature, privacy and space. War over, in the personal columns of *The Times*, they find their idyll.

The house is in Kent built in Tudor times by Flemish weavers with the curved gables of their homeland. It has 33 rooms, a resident bat, a temperamental insatiable geriatric boiler and five kitchens. It is home to lilacs and roses and swallows in the stable. Over the years, its powers of seduction ensnare not just the small band of Londoners but also a succession of domestic staff, weekend visitors, foreign paying guests and tenants. The whole is presided over by the magnificent figure of Howard, the head gardener.

Howard had served the previous owner, the Colonel, beginning as a page boy. He marries the kitchen maid and the pair rise through the ranks. As cook, she is renowned for her crab apple jelly and artichoke soup. After the Colonel's death and on behalf of the trustees, Howard has tended the empty house through the long years of the war. He confides to Ruth,

"I fixed for you to have it but don't you say nothing to nobody . . ." "Don't you say nothing . . ." is Howard's favourite opener to every conversation with Ruth which usually concerns him fixing something: leaks, the boiler, the Colonel's daughter seeking return of linoleum, fire extinguishers and the Cox's apple trees (the latter without success).

Ruth decides Howard understands that her group has "no ambition to masquerade as the squirearchy", instead, "we longed for the good life of the English country . . . the pinnacle of domesticity". Domesticity up to a point, she discovers.

While the other residents earn a wage necessary to pay for the lease, Ruth slaves, clocking up 126 hours a week, on the land, in the house, in the dark pokey scullery with its back breaking sink where she imagines many a scullery maid must have spent her whole day washing up for her "betters" above stairs. The dream of rural life begins to splinter as Ruth fails to fulfil all her tasks, "the rooms became thick with dust, baths sticky with tide marks."

Ruth Adam was an extraordinary woman. A former teacher, she was a feminist and a socialist. She wrote radio plays, several novels, most concerning social issues such as the plight of girls in care. She also wrote two long running strips in *Girl* comic, about young women who were brave, resourceful and clever. Her final work, *A Woman's Place*, a history of women's lives in the twentieth century was published in 1975. She died two years later.

A House in the Country is enchanting, wise and funny. It is set at a time when the country is in transition moving from the pre-war deferential, class conscious society of "us" and "them" to the birth of the N.H.S. and the welfare state and "an exhilarating feeling that we were launched on a new world". The novel is a cameo of those times, full of snapshots of the social and political contradictions, as the past drags hard on the present.

Soon after the London group arrive, for instance, Howard takes Ruth for a private conversation to the greenhouse, illicitly kept warm through the war. What flowers would she like "for the table this summer"? Democratically, Ruth attempts to engage Howard in consultation. He is firm: "The mistress always decides the flowers".

In another example, Howard despises the nearby village and all its occupants for unclear reasons – rural idylls always have their mysterious feuds and enmities. Undaunted, the Londoners visit the local pub, and meet with "the bristling hostility proper towards newcomers in the country". However, the hostility persists. It emerges that it's because Ruth's daughter Jane has been sent to the local primary school and that is considered no place for "a child of the manor".

Gradually, Ruth, metaphorically haunted by the ghost of the little scullery maid, comes to a realisation. "I began to think our experiment did not deserve to succeed. . . . the gracious life in the front wing, after all, depended entirely upon service in the back wing, and it didn't seem a justifiable way of living".

The spell, however, is hard to break. Colin, aged four, receives a countryman's apprenticeship from Howard. Howard shows him how "to wring a chicken's neck . . . kill snakes in the long grass, use a bill hook on nettles and build a hen house from discarded wood. . . . Every boy should have a year at the heels of an old craftsman sometime in his life."

In addition, there are the unfolding seasons. Adam is striking in her imagery: "narcissi were treading on the heels of the daffodils; primrose queueing for attention in the grass". Ruth's domestic burden is eased when maids, Mollie and Noah arrive and expertly take over the running of the house. Labour minister, Barbara Castle (one of many exotic weekend guests) advises on their terms and conditions – a forty hour week, double pay for overtime. Adams writes, "The ghost of the little scullery maid was laid at last."

Over the eight years, the group disbands, Ruth and her husband try alternative sources of income such as renting out half the manor and Howard retires, choosing as his successor Morris on the basis of the lashing tongue of Morris's wife. The ideal situation for the gardens is "a scold in the gardener's cottage and an eternally pottering exile outside it."

Eventually, a decision has to be taken. New tenants are found. The Adams make a bonfire of the furniture and contents they are unable to sell or give away and the villagers assume they have set fire to the manor. Back in London and for months after, the couple struggle to pay off their debts. "The manor stretched out her hand and kept us enslaved," Ruth Adam writes.

Her memories have turned sour but such is her skill, the manor's rural spell for readers remains intact.

Yvonne Roberts

1

THIS is a cautionary tale, and true.

Never fall in love with a house. The one we fell in love with wasn't even ours. If she had been, she would have ruined us just the same. We found out some things about her afterwards, among them what she did to that poor old parson, back in the eighteen-seventies. If we had found them out earlier . . . ? It wouldn't have made any difference. We were in that maudlin state when reasonable argument is quite useless. Our old parents tried it. We wouldn't listen. "If you could only *see* her," we said.

She first came into our lives through the Personal Column of *The Times*. I have the advertisement still. Sometimes I look at it bitterly, as if it were an old dance-programme, with some scrawled initials on it which I had since learned to hate.

Why did I have to read the Personal Column that particular morning? It isn't any use, really, trying to blame the unkind gods. I was studying it every day, looking for this very house.

It was the end of the war, and we were very tired of squalor. We were tired of the black-out edging obscuring the daylight from the windows and of breakfasts of powdered egg eaten at noon because one had been fire-watching last night. We were so very tired of disorder—of living in one room to save fuel, of the smell of scraps boiling up for the backyard hens, of beds in the downstairs rooms and of a grubby air-raid shelter in the tiny neglected garden.

We had our dream of escape. It was the standard, classic dream of every English town-dweller. It was the dream of country life, in which everything is transformed. In the country, the sun would shine all the time and we would be wakened by birds instead of sirens. Country people were simple and gentle and golden-hearted. It is an everlasting dream, left over from some forgotten forefather before the Industrial Revolution. All around us, the Londoners are dreaming it still, though we have awakened.

The porter in our block of flats has been looking, these twenty years, for a country job. I asked him this morning just what he thought he was going to get out of it that was so wonderful. He said, "To smell the grass." People on the city housing list admit shyly, "What we'd *really* like would be the country." Parents who make sacrifices for their children's education rate the sacrifice of the dream above everything else. "If we didn't have to pay school-fees, we could have a weekend cottage in the country."

When the English get to heaven, they will make trouble if they find it, as advertised, a golden city. What they bargained for—Saint Peter must have seen it plenty of times on Christmas cards—was something with thatch and lavender and rambler roses, or something with a cobbled stableyard, an orchard and singing birds.

There was nothing unusual about our dream. It was just like everyone else's, except that there were six of us—not counting the children—weaving the same one all at once. Also, we put in more than average time on our day-dreaming, because we talked of it always in the air-raid shelter, always on trains that were held up, always in queues, and any other time when everyday life was more sordid and boring than usual. Between us, our dream country house became so real that we began to think it must exist somewhere, in real bricks and mortar, with real grass and apple-trees and wistaria over the door.

We were one of those groups that grew up all over Britain in the days of evacuation and billeting and sleeping in the suburbs to avoid air-raid noises. Bob, who was my brother, turned up at our house after the fall of France, when we had given him up for dead, and went on turning up there again from Ireland and Portugal and Egypt and India until presently we forgot that there had been any interval between the nursery we used to share at home, and the nursery to which he was uncle. Lefty and he had shared a peace-time establishment, so Lefty moved his civilian kit in with Bob's and presently it began to be an accepted fact of life that he lived with us when he was on leave. He was in the Navy and Bob in the Air Force. Timmy had been at college with my husband and was godfather to our eldest son. He was one of the golden-voiced hierarchy at the B.B.C. When he was bombed out, he moved himself and such possessions as survived into our spare bedroom. Diana had been doing walking-on parts at the local rep when we were first married and was godmother to another of the children. Now she got West-end parts, and moved in with us because of air-raids. We were not particularly congenial to each other, but we were used to being together by now. We had worn paper caps in the air-raid shelter, to distract the children and concocted ways of keeping warm, and shared secrets—such as the name of a shop where you could buy marzipan which gave you the illusion of eating sweets. We knew that we wanted to get away from the shaming petty disputes which blew up among us, about who had taken more than his share of butter, but it never crossed our minds that we should get away from each other. We had planned our dream of country living for so long that we seemed bound together, whether we liked it or not, because we were all involved. We should go on being together, but we should be orderly. We should breakfast at a fixed hour, all looking clean and tidy, with the windows open to let the fresh country dawn float in. Lefty used to dwell affectionately on this bit of the dream. He was in one of the Little Ships and hated breakfast, crammed in a tiny cabin with two other officers, none of them having bathed, worse than the night's action which had preceded it.

Our rooms would be tidy, we wouldn't borrow each other's clothes and the day would be marked out in patches of routine that had gone on for so many generations that we should simply slip into the well-trodden path and follow it.

"After dinner, in the evenings," said Diana. "We shall all sit round in the old drawing-room, with the French windows open and night-scented stock in the flower-bed outside, and sip our coffee." Diana thought most about this, because she hated queueing for spam in a smoky restaurant after her play, and then going out through the black-out to catch a dawdling train home, worse than the flying bombs which invariably (she said) spoiled her best lines.

"Log-fires in every room," said Timmy.

"Cutting down trees for them at the week-end," said Bob.

My husband and I thought privately of our children having the kind of life which is the pinnacle of English childhood—a whole domain of gardens, shrubbery, stables, barn and secret lairs that no one else can ever find. We didn't say it aloud, because the others might have thought we were only subscribing to the plan for the sake of what our children could get out of it at everyone else's expense. They would, as a matter of fact, have been dead right.

"It must be one of those houses that's been built, bit by bit, for hundreds of years," said Timmy.

"It must have great windows that let all the sunlight in."

"It must have so much space that we never use half of it."

"It must have acres and acres of garden."

"Dozens of outhouses."

"It ought to have a river running through the garden," said Lefty, whose fishing-rods and guns were stored away in his boyhood home in the smoky north.

"It ought to have a ghost," said Timmy. But I wouldn't agree to the ghost because of the children.

"They'll be fast asleep in the nursery wing, right out of hearing of the rest of the house," said Timmy wistfully. In our present crowded quarters he was sleeping next to the new baby. He was broadcasting to Occupied Europe, which kept him up late, and resented losing more sleep, though otherwise he was very public-spirited about the baby. Once he had come home in an air-raid, from a safe spot on the other side of London because he had remembered I should be alone and couldn't carry three children to the shelter at once. Apart from this, our relations were poisoned by his believing that I let the Irish domestic help herself from his sugar ration when he wasn't home.

"There'll be three or four kitchens, with red-flagged floors and hams hanging from the ceiling and we shan't have to live in any of them," I contributed. We were all sitting huddled round the stove in our uncomfortable little suburban one, and could still smell everything that had been cooked in it that day, including the hens' mash. "Each bedroom will have a dressing-room so that there's no more of this First Up, Best Dressed," Lefty added broodingly. It was true that Timmy, who shared his bedroom, did help himself to Lefty's civilian clothes when he ran short, and also left them at the B.B.C. when he came home in a hurry.

Our next-door neighbours on the right launched on one of their party evenings, with screams of maniacal laughter. Our next-door neighbours on the left called in to ask if we knew that the children had dragged their black-out curtain right away from the window.

"Above all," we decided, "It must stand alone. Not another house within half a mile, at the very least. There must be miles and miles of green fields, washing right up to its garden walls."

We babbled of green fields.

"It can't be true," we said, reading the Personal Column. "Either someone's put it in for a joke, or else it's really a code message, or else there's some immense snag about the place."

We went down to Kent to view it, in turns, and came back looking as if we had been to Lyonesse.

We never had a moment's doubt. It would have been strange if we had. We added our incomes together and found that we could afford it. We were angry with our lawyers for even wanting to discuss the lease. "They don't *realize,*" we said to each other privately. But when it was all finally settled for Ladyday, we were satisfied. That would be the beginning of Spring and the end of the long, long winter that had gone on since September 1939. Lefty and Bob were sure that Monty would get the peace signed in time for them to help with the moving in. Timmy said that while Occupied Europe was celebrating liberation, they wouldn't want to hear his voice, which would leave him free to unload the vans and lay carpets. Diana, whose play had been running for a long time, grew gleeful as audiences began to fall off round about the new year.

"I'll be out of a job by March," she prophesied. "Perhaps I'd better take over the housekeeping when we get to the manor, then you could spend all your time on the children. I know about managing staff from the stage-hands at the theatre."

One of our regular disputes was about whether we lived in such cheerless squalor because supplies were bad or because I was a bad housekeeper. I was sick and tired of war-time housekeeping, but only over my dead body would Diana have taken the reins. They all thought that I was so determined to keep the keys and ration-books myself only so that I could be sure the children got the best of everything. It was true, too. But once we got among the farms where the milk came from, and the hens were laying, and we had a gardener bringing in a basket full of fresh produce every morning, I meant to reform and dole out fair shares all round.

"I suppose you'll wash all the clothes at home when you've got that clothes-line on the river bank to dry them," said

Timmy, when the laundry failed to return his shirt and he couldn't take one of Lefty's because Lefty was home on leave.

I said that when we were all living an orderly, disciplined life, with formal meals, I should require wage-slaves of some sort. They all looked amazed, because it had been patriotic now, for a long time, to be a downtrodden housewife, and the more downtrodden the more patriotic.

"Besides, you just got Biddy over from Ireland," Timmy argued.

"But you say you each want two private rooms and roses on the polished oak table and clean sheets every week smelling of lavender. Biddy and I can't do all that and clean the thirty-three rooms as well."

In the end I was bought off by a promise to keep on the gardener's boy as well as the old gardener who went with the lease. It wouldn't have been any use standing out for more, because you couldn't get domestic help. I had only got Biddy's labour permit because of the new baby, and she was only staying because she had married a parachutist (which had been the real object of her crossing the Irish Channel) and thought she might as well stay where she was until he came home.

We began to count the months.

"No smoky fogs in Kent," said Timmy, winding a scarf round his mouth to protect his voice.

"He won't cry at night when he's had country air all day," said my husband, when the baby woke us.

"It's going to be a relief dealing at a nice, friendly, respectful little village shop," said Diana, coming back from the town in a rage with the grocer.

We began to count the weeks.

Our furniture was going to look pretty silly, spread over four times the area.

"When I was bombed out, I gave the studio furniture that was left to a friend to look after," said Timmy. "I'll get it back."

Bob had made one of his extraordinary and complex arrangements, while he was in India on Mountbatten's staff, to have some carpets shipped home to him through diplomatic channels.

"They ought to arrive by the time we move," he said. "There's a lot of mosquito netting as well. That will do to make into something."

Diana mused about getting hold of some of the stage props when her play folded up, and Lefty said there were two seats out of a wrecked flying-boat lying in a store shed at his naval base. We used to sit for hours with a plan of the house before us, distributing our inadequate furniture and effects over the vast spaces. At the last moment, Lefty brought home a bicycle which he had fished out of the bottom of Poole harbour.

"The very thing for going errands to the village," he said. "It's only a bit rusty with sea-water."

We asked if he had found a body with it, but he said he hadn't looked.

The last month was spent in sordid disputes. Our landlord had gone bankrupt, and also to jail which seemed to make everything more difficult, not less. We quarrelled with his wife about whether the worm had been in the wood when we arrived or whether we had brought them with us, and with the new tenants as to who was to pay for the bathroom window-latch. We quarrelled with the Town Hall as to whether moving our pile of after-packing rubbish came under the heading of services from the rates or an extra. Timmy conducted an acrimonious correspondence with the friend who had his furniture, as to whether she should pay for hiring it or he for having it stored. They finally settled that Timmy should buy it back from her at its original price. We couldn't understand why, when we were so happy, other people should think it worth while to nag about things that didn't really matter.

"Once all this is over, we'll never have anything in our lives like this again," we vowed. And we thought of the people we were dealing with over the manor—the civil and obliging agent, the gentle, respectful old gardener, and the Trustees, all scholarly and courteous old gentlemen without a "g" to end a word among them. "You simply can't *imagine* yourself ever having a slanging match with any of them," we agreed.

"Only a month to go now," we said. "Only a week, three days, two days—this time tomorrow."

It was unbelievable that the day should really be here, because I had waited for it—not merely since we saw *The Times* advertisement, but since I was a child, lying in bed and watching the shaft of light from the hall gas across the nursery ceiling.

My childhood was spent in draughty Vicarages, where ends never quite met. And I knew, ever since I could remember, that my mother had been brought up in a different kind of house—with a drive sweeping up to a pillared door, where great trees stood sentinel. I knew, from occasional visits to my grandfather, how there was a dairy with slate slabs next to the harness-room, with its smell of saddle-soap, and also how the household moved to a measured routine, like the figures of an old-fashioned dance. My mother had married a penniless curate and annoyed her family even more by being blissfully and unrepentantly happy with him. But I knew that one part of her was always homesick for the traditional ways of her old home. She would pass an expert, knowing hand over the grocer's horse at the back door, and set out the heavy silver and fine linen of her trousseau when we had the churchwardens to supper. It was half a joke and half a secret between us that when I was married I was going to have just such a house and invite her to stay with us there. After thirteen years of putting her up on a sofa in flats, and in Diana's narrow slip of a back bedroom here, I was at last going to see our plan come true.

They say that when a stranger's face seems familiar, it is because it is like a forgotten face of your childhood. I don't know if it is true about people. But I know it is about houses. When I stood, for the first time in my life, in the hall of the manor, it was not strange to me. It was the house I had promised to have, so that my mother could come and stay in it.

The furniture-vans drove away, with the others waving to me from the tail-board. I put the three children to bed in a boarding-house up the road and went back to clear up.

I had never been entirely alone in this house since the war began, and it felt terribly empty. Now that it was cleared of our possessions, I seemed to be looking right across the six years of war, back to the time when it had been empty before. All the things that had happened since then seemed to fill the deserted rooms, as though they had been buried beneath our everyday possessions and were freed to float about now like the dust from beneath the carpets. As I swept, I remembered starting a canteen here for the Local Defence Volunteers. I remembered a stranded unit of soldiers sleeping all over the floors, the night my new-born nephew first fell fatally ill. I remembered, in the lonely silence, how I had searched among sleeping bodies for the doctor and how he had risen at once, without a sigh or a question. I remembered the night my second child was born here, when I wondered if I had brought him into the world to be a German serf, and the night the third was born, when I thought I had brought him into a world which was going to be new and better than ever before. I remembered sitting on the stairs with him, shaking, at the sound of the first flying bomb. It seemed as if the house had always been dark like this, and as if we had always been lightened, and tragedy always on the doorstep. It seemed as if the whole six years had been one long, dark, weary and monotonous night. Then the air-raid siren went and I locked up and went back to the children. I didn't even look back as I closed the gate, and I never went back to the house again.

Tomorrow was another day.

2

On Ladyday the sun shone and none of the small white clouds floating about crossed its face for a single moment. There were so many daffodils that we kept looking at them again to make sure we weren't seeing double. They were so thick along the back drive that we couldn't tell how many people had slipped in the back gate to steal them each day. It seemed a pity even to walk in the orchard because you couldn't help treading them underfoot. We had tea in the garden when the vans were unloaded, and the removal men sat staring around them, speechless, as they sipped theirs.

We couldn't sleep for the birds. At dawn, there was first a clearing of throats, a few tuning-notes, and one or two experimental phrases tried over. Then, with a burst, came the symphony and we got up and began to unpack the crates.

There were heavy Georgian shutters on all the windows and when they were folded back, with a clang of their iron bars, the sunshine flooded in. Every hinge and handle in the place worked perfectly; every lock turned without a squeak.

"I like to keep things right," said Howard, the old gardener who had been let with the place.

He had been with the old Colonel, the last owner, since he was a page-boy in buttons and was still the same size as he had been then. His life was a success story that had gone on too long. He graduated from page to under-gardener and married the kitchen-maid. The kitchen-maid became cook and he became head gardener. They stayed at that eminence while the establishment crumbled away beneath them.

The Colonel died and ruled a final line under a family tree which had flourished in the manor ever since the Flemish weavers, homesick for the country which had cast them out, had touched up the Kentish landscape with the curved gables they used to know back home. Howard stayed on in his cottage, guarding the great empty house from German airmen, rushing busily towards London. Every night he went round it closing the shutters. Every morning he let the daylight in again, though there was no one to see it.

It had dawned on him as his footsteps echoed so loudly in the corridors that he had to stop and listen for buzz-bombs, that times had changed and would never change back again. It was in the grip of this revelation that he had decided to let us have the house.

"The Trustees leave everything to me," he said. "They know that agent doesn't know nothing about the place." He despised the agent, who had never known the manor in its heyday, and who was a quiet little Welshman, living a tidy life between his office and his modest home. Howard spoke with respect of the predecessor, who had been a tweedy cad with a moustache and riding-whip, and who had married the daughter of a county family at a shot-gun wedding. "She wept at the altar," said Howard admiringly. "He led her a life afterwards, too."

"They told me to fix up with a suitable tenant," said Howard. "I fixed for you to have it, but don't you say nothing to anybody about that. It'll be all right as long as you don't mention it."

Always, he retired into a cloud of secrecy to end a conversation. Over and over again we wondered why he had let us have the manor. The explanation was so simple that I didn't stumble on it for years. He knew—this bustling little upper servant, left over into an age when his kind was obsolete—just why we wanted it. He knew, as if he could see into our hearts, that we longed for the good life of the English country house. He knew we had no ambition to masquerade as the squirearchy, but that we longed for the satisfying routine that is the pinnacle of British domesticity. He had looked over the mixed group that came down, one by one, to view the place and decided that we could be welded into a makeshift, post-war imitation of the establishment he had always known.

He told us that he had awarded us the manor over the head of a very distinguished Brigadier and his wife. She had put herself out of the running by murmuring something about turning her dressing-room into a bathroom.

"What a silly suggestion," we said to each other, smugly. Years later, as I drew a bucket of water out of the river in order to wash up, I realized just how silly it had been.

Howard had kept the bolts oiled and had lighted fires in the echoing rooms to keep the damp out, but he hadn't been able to prevent the walls from fading and letting great sheets of paper peel off and bow despondently towards the floor.

"They weren't really what we should have chosen anyway," we consoled each other. The Colonel had liked crimson with black lines better than anything, but we couldn't make out on what basis he had chosen brown cabbages or pale-grey disembodied leaves for the rest of the walls. We decided that he must have sent for countless books of samples and gone through them, carefully choosing only the ones that he could be certain no one else could possibly select.

At that time it was forbidden by law to spend any money on re-decorating a house.

"And that agent can't do nothing about it," added Howard, implying that the moustachioed cad had known his way around the law.

We put on our old Civil Defence overalls and whitewashed the walls from attic to cellar. We were in that state of honey-moon enchantment when we kept on calling each other to look what we had achieved. The picture began to take shape. As the walls grew white, the old wood grew blacker. The carved crest on the staircase seemed to emerge from its background and become visible, as though someone had wheeled a television camera up towards it. In the dining-hall, four carved wooden heads stood out as the four evangelists and the Dutch tiles in the fireplace as Bible scenes. The Adam fireplace in the drawing-room, on the contrary, receded, its ivory merging into the white, so that you found yourself absently tracing its curves with your fingers, as you warmed your hands before the blazing logs.

Those first few days, we barely set foot in the garden at all, though the spring was positively battering at the windows. Howard used to come in to see that we were not doing anything which the Colonel would not have approved.

"The ladies have the lighter hand on the brushes," he would say, pontifically. Diana's manipulation round a moulded edge put him in mind of the Colonel's wife, who had the lightest touch on the reins he ever saw in any lady. Diana turned pink with pleasure, because we knew by now that the Colonel's lady had been so fascinating that he had wooed and married her in the teeth of two families' opposition and fresh from sowing his wild oats. Between the oats and the wedding he had sold immense chunks of the estate his forefathers had so carefully garnered. But Howard said positively that she was worth it. Our imaginations boggled at trying to picture any female who, in Howard's eyes, could possibly come up to that standard.

But now he was left with a post-war Utility substitute for her, in the shape of myself, he was determined to make the best of it. He was a castaway from another world, washed up on the unpromising shore at the other side of the Second World War, and instead of lamenting the past, was prepared to build with such material as came to hand. The second morning after we arrived, he was shocked because he found me cleaning the children's shoes.

"That won't do," he said. "Don't you say nothing to anybody, and I'll see what I can manage." It was arranged that the gardener's boy, Ernest, should double for the missing knife-and-boot boy. Howard explained to me privately that it was because Ernest was only ninepence-in-the-shilling mentally that he could put over on him such a monstrous imposition. Gardeners' boys did not clean shoes, any more than knife-and-boot boys were expected to weed the paths. We were amused among ourselves at the secrecy veiling the arrangement until we discovered that we were, in fact, breaking an identical taboo of 1945. Persons employed in gardening (food production) were not supposed to be used for in-door labour (domestic).

The manor had the look of a monastery, with its white walls and polished floors and bare rooms. Howard produced a jar of beeswax from his own bees, and Diana and I wound rags thickly around our shoes and skated all over the floors with folded arms, as I had seen the maids do in Spain. We used to have the radio on, so that we could do it in time to the music. It was an agreeable exercise and the floors began to get the warm, *living* look which old wood gets when it has outlived generations of human polishers. All the old wood in the house began to come to life in the same way. The Trustees had left us three refectory tables and two Sheraton cupboards and some carved chairs and chests, because they were too big to store anywhere and were entailed, so could not be sold. We were glad our own furniture was so sparse. We loved the great empty spaces and bare floors and arched alcoves without any ornament to distract from their curves.

All the same, we needed chairs and tables if we were not to be reduced to taking them with us from room to room.

That summer of 1945 was the worst time in history for buying furniture. You couldn't get anything new, except on dockets. Diana toyed with the idea of marrying a stage-door-johnnie who was always asking her, because if you got married you got a whole lot of dockets at once.

"You could use some of them to buy yourself a proper Utility bed," we coaxed her. She had bought herself a second-hand bed and mattress, but had taken against them because one morning she woke up and found a whole lot of young creatures wriggling out of the mattress into the blanket.

But she decided that it would be too tiresome having to have the masher at the manor sometimes. A passing suggestion that she should marry Lefty was strangely received. They darted a furtive glance at each other and changed the subject.

Second-hand furniture was scarce and fantastically dear. The grocers and butchers were beginning to practise an occasional intermittent civility towards customers, in case it might ever be needed, but the junk-shop-dealers had taken over the dictatorship. The junk-shop that could have been most useful to us, in the local market-town, was packed from floor to ceiling with bits of china, old wash-stands, grubby pieces of matting and broken slices of linoleum, marked at about the price of Persian rugs. We were continually seeing something at the back of the edifice which was just what we wanted.

"I can't get it down today. You'll have to wait," said the junk-man.

"But we want to buy it," we wailed.

"On Friday week," he said patiently, "I mean to have a clean-up and tidy the shop. If you'll come back then, I'll see if I can reach it down for you."

We used to storm out of the shop, vowing revenge. I got it, too, to the uttermost farthing, but not for seven years.

We made a discovery. Our manor was built to take furniture too unwieldy for any other house. Mirrors that the pawnshop seemed to have been built around were squeezed out of the door and dragged triumphantly home. When we put them up, they looked like postage-stamps on the empty pages of a large album. Lefty bought a cupboard which required three men to move it, aided by rollers. The dealer had given up the idea of ever selling it, and had to turn out all his stock from it and arrange that round the shop instead. It certainly made Lefty's room look less empty, but there didn't seem to be any use for it.

"It would do for guns," said Lefty.

"But you said you only had two. They'll be lost in it."

"I could buy some more. They ought to be going cheap now the fighting's over."

We discovered auction-sales. I learned to copy the farmers' wives and go round the sale-room the day before, unrolling piles of linen and curtains and examining, tight-lipped, the extent of rents and worn patches. The sales followed a pattern. In the morning, the dealers came down from London and bought up old silver for the Americans. After that, we progressed steadily down-hill, through recognizable articles of furniture to "Lots" that were classified under associations only comprehended by the auctioneers' men. By tea-time, only the disagreeable junk-man and myself would be left, glaring at each other over piles of bamboo tables and commodes. Once I brought home a piano.

"But none of us can play," they chorused ungratefully.

"The children can learn."

"But you only went there to buy fire-irons."

"The fire-irons were in the same Lot."

"It's a sheer waste of money."

I knew it. But it had been worth four guineas to see the defeated face of the junk-man, who had really wanted it. After a time we got used to seeing it in a corner. It was quite a pretty piano, with a picture inset above the keyboard and a far-away tinkling noise when you struck the keys. If ever a piano had a success-story that one had, because having shared a four-guinea bid with fire-irons, it was played on, in the years to come, by Ernest Lush and Rafael Kubelik.

Sometimes I found the auction-sales saddening. The whole contents of a home, second-hand, look quite different from any model establishment set out to attract buyers in a furniture-store. The things that must have been favourites of the family were the very ones sneered at by all of us prospective buyers as we poked round. I couldn't understand how any one could let a worn child's crib, and little chair, and old dolls and trains be exposed in public for the sake of the few shillings they would bring. I began to understand why the sale of the old home was such a sure-fire tragic scene in any Victorian novel.

"It must be terribly painful and humiliating," I said, as we turned over a pile of old photographs, looking for frames of the size we wanted, and jeering at the present occupants. If anyone had told me then that before very long I should be eagerly counting the shillings brought in by my own household goods, I simply shouldn't have believed it.

"If you've got a moment," said Howard. "I'd like to speak to you privately."

I left the others whitewashing and followed him down the garden. While we had been arranging the house, the spring had really broken out. The wistaria hung in pale clusters over her own bare brown twigs; the narcissi had begun to compete with the daffodils. Between the drive and the field fence the celandines were blazing gold. I never knew, before I went to the manor, how many different shades of green exist. Primroses were thick among the grass; there were violets at the foot of the trees. Right up on the long lawn, under a great oak-tree, there was a complete ring of wild orchids. The river ran high and brown between its banks where this year's grass was struggling up among last year's dead leaves. I followed Howard down to the stableyard in a daze. Opposite the stables was a little greenhouse. It was warm inside and there was a heavy scent. He had some great Madonna lilies blooming there.

"Don't say nothing," he said. "I kept a bit of a fire on all winter from ashes that were lying about. They wouldn't let us have a permit to heat greenhouses."

"It's the flowers," he said, after he had closed the greenhouse door with us both inside. "I just wanted to know what you'd want for the table this summer."

I felt like a downtrodden princess who has suddenly been promoted to the throne and found herself implored to state her wishes. It was incredible, after years with a few mournful blossoms from the local shop to be asked what I would have grown for me.

"Perhaps I'd better consult the others."

"The mistress always decides the flowers," said Howard positively.

I cast a fleeting look at our agreements to share and share alike and seized my opportunity.

"Sweet-peas," I said.

We had never had enough sweet-peas at the Vicarage. Every year, my mother used to beg the gardener-cum-verger to have another try, but they always turned out rather twisted and puny. This year, when she came to stay, she should have her room full of them.

"And the colours?" asked Howard briskly.

"I like the dark ones."

"I know where I can pick up some black," said Howard.

But when I got back to the house there was a telephone-call to say my mother was dead.

When I went off to the funeral, Howard brought me all the Madonna lilies, cut and packed most beautifully for the journey.

All the loveliness of that first spring at the manor turned heavy with grief.

The hawthorns whitened on the hedges and the chestnut-trees raised their candles, rows and rows of them, in red and ivory. The orchard was always a little world of floating blossom, as though someone had shaken it up like a snowstorm imprisoned in a glass ball. The air was full of country sounds—cows lowing, a dog barking in the farm across the fields, lambs bleating and the cuckoo, very close by, in the trees beside the river. The baby learned to walk on the wide, soft stretches of grass. The children grew brown and bright-eyed, slept when the dusk came down and woke again with the dawn. But it all seemed to be set in a minor key.

Then the magnolia bloomed.

Hundreds and hundreds of huge waxy tulips towered above the slim black trunk. People stopped their cars at the gate to ask if they might come and look at it. We half-turned our heads as they came up and then turned back to staring at it ourselves again.

It was like the backcloth of an opera. If it had been a painted one, it would have been just silly. But because it was real, it took your breath away.

At night, before we went to bed, we all went out and looked at it again. We couldn't believe that we had really seen what we had been picturing to ourselves as we ate our supper. But in the moonlight it was more astonishing still. It was almost oppressive. Such a tree has no right in a Kentish garden. It was like fetching a goddess from the isles of Greece over and dumping her down at a village social. We shivered a little, as we looked at it in the moonlight. There was a chill in the air.

Next morning, the frost had struck. Down the whole of the north side, where the cold wind had touched the tree, every blossom was shrivelled brown and destroyed. She looked crippled. It was a relief when the rest of the tulips had dropped off and when she drew her large green leaves over the naked wreck of her beauty. We thought sorrowfully that we had wasted several of her twelve hours of perfection indoors, where we couldn't see her.

3

WE GOT the manor arranged.

It was one of those country houses which has been built to live in and not to impress passers-by. Ever since the Flemish weavers put their new wealth into making their home life a noble thing, Kent has been sprinkled with houses which dignify everyday life. The manor had been started in Tudor times and added to regularly until Victoria was dead. But each father of the family, in his turn, had wanted the same thing—more room in which to conduct the pleasant, orderly family life of a country manor. Therefore, the building of each generation fitted on to the building of the previous one. They had thought differently about the height of ceilings and the size of rooms and the kind of bricks to use. But because their object had been the same, the great building was one harmonious whole. Also, each generation of builders had faithfully held to the curved, Dutch-looking gables with which the manor had started. In the garden, close to Howard's cottage, was a second cottage, with mysterious inhabitants about whom Howard had forbidden us to talk, even among ourselves. But we did observe quietly to each other, that although it was a modest affair, built within living memory, someone had thought it worth while to shape its roof as the very first manor roof had been shaped, long and long ago.

The manor was a hollow square, built around a little cobbled courtyard. At eight o'clock every Saturday morning, the ninepence-in-the-shilling garden boy unlocked the inner door and swept it with a yard-broom and then locked the door again for another week.

The south wing had the family rooms and the east wing the largest and grandest ones—the great dining-hall and the Best Guest above it, which looked out on to rolling lawns and a copper-beech tree. The New Wing, which was the north one, had servants' quarters. There were five main kitchens and four smaller service rooms. The west wing had sewing-rooms, preserving-rooms, and the lady's maid's room. Howard explained to us that they had been obliged to build her a room half-way between servants and family because that was her place in the hierarchy. Bob chose that room for his own because it had a great iron bar, running right across the ceiling, on which he could drape his mosquito-nets if he wanted to.

"That's where she used to hang the crinoline dresses," Howard explained.

Every bedroom had a dressing-room. We all became remarkably tidy. You wouldn't have known our bedrooms as belonging to the same people who had once had coats flung on the bed and overflowing suitcases on all the chairs. The house imposed order upon us, whether we liked it or not. When you have thirty-three rooms, you feel obliged to keep something in each one, and the possessions which had filled the little suburban house to bursting-point now vanished quietly into the depths of the manor.

Lefty took the Best Guest, which was the largest of all, because he was so tired of a tiny little cabin. But with his bed one end of it, and his cupboard the other, he said he got an uneasy delusion of being out-of-doors, between sea and sky, every morning when he woke. However, it had taken so long to whitewash that he thought he might as well stay in it and get something back for all the labour.

Timmy surprised us by settling in the servants' wing. I think it was because that was the most recently-built and his studio furniture looked more at home in the plain square rooms there than among the arched ceilings and mullioned windows in the old part. Howard congratulated him on having unerringly chosen the Cook's Bedroom, which was naturally the pick of the wing. Long after we had settled in, we found the thirty-third room by accident. It had a door hidden in a dark corner of the front landing. Behind the door was a curving staircase and at the top of the staircase a little attic right among the jig-saw of old roofs. If you leaned out on a Saturday morning, you could just see the head of the gardener's boy as he swept below. Bob built a model railway in it, with mountains and tunnels and hillside villages, which, over the years became so famous that railway officials used to come down to see it and get new ideas to apply to their own work.

Diana had the Second-Best-Guest and we had the Colonel's rooms. The children had the old nurseries, but Howard told us that a little room over the wistaria had always been, by tradition, the domain of the daughter of the house, so we put Jane in there. It was an exquisite little room, with mullioned windows and a mirror built in over the fireplace exactly the right height for a little girl. We put aside the whitewash when we came to it, and painted it the palest of powder-blue, with the ceiling a pink so pale that you were never quite certain whether it was the sunset reflected or distemper. We hung curtains of faded blue chintz, with small pink roses on them, and round the walls we put portraits of little girls of long ago in their best clothes.

Bob had Eastern carpets from end to end of his room and mosquito-netting in the windows, Diana had orange and green stripes bought from a stage set, we had the furniture bought for our very first flat, Lefty had the curtains from the captain's cabin and two leather seats from a flying-boat, and Timmy had his studio divan and some pictures painted by an artist friend which would certainly have surprised the Colonel. But for our guest-room, which had once been a chapel, and which looked out on to the magnolia tree itself, we all gave up the best of everything we had.

"Have you ever wondered exactly who we're doing all this for?" Timmy asked, as we stood round in the finished guest-room admiring the effect.

Hefty and Bob began to murmur about ravishing girl-friends they meant to have down for week-ends and then stopped because Diana was looking chilly. Timmy, who disliked his own family profoundly, added that he hoped that no one had any idea about inviting their relatives, because it was not for that he had given up his only fireside chair.

"The room rates a film-star at least," said Diana.

"We ought to ask a world-famous poet when the magnolia is in bloom, then he could write an ode to it," I suggested.

Timmy had been thinking it over.

"If we're ever going to have enough money to support this house in the style to which she's been accustomed, we're all going to have to do a whole lot better in our various jobs," he said.

We all murmured agreement. It has been, after all, the reason for making a fortune, from the Flemish weavers to the latest industrial magnate who becomes M.F.H., English trade and industry owe their very existence to the ambition to have a country house and live in it.

"We must all get a lot more ambitious," Timmy went on. "We've got to think about getting to know people who can be useful to us. We ought to ask them down. That's what you do at country-house week-ends. All sorts of big deals get settled, between Friday night and Monday morning. That's the kind of thing we ought to aim at."

"One of the Press Lords, for instance?" suggested my husband, brightening up.

"Just so. Or a millionaire."

"Or an international impresario."

"Or a film-director."

"Or a distinguished politician, belonging to the party in power."

"We ought to have some people with titles sometimes, to please Howard."

"But occasionally we ought to take in a homeless tramp or someone like that, so that he can describe it in his autobiography."

We were all silent, looking out on to the leafy magnolia and thinking it over. We didn't doubt that we could achieve it. After all, we had made our combined dream, woven in the dismal days of war-time, come true so far, down to the smallest detail. If enough of you plan a dream, and believe in it faithfully, you can make it come alive, like Galatea. We had invented the manor, among ourselves, in the air-raid shelter, and here we were living in her, with the log fires and panelling and the river running through the garden and the green fields washing up to the garden fence. We thought we could achieve this new extension of the plan, and we were right. Every single one of our dream-guests slept in the Magnolia Room before we left it to strangers. We had only left one thing out of our calculations, from the very beginning. That was the old familiar legend about people whose wishes were granted and who lived to wish that they had been refused instead.

So far, we had lived a self-contained life on our little island of house and gardens among the fields. Now we had arranged the house, and Howard had returned to the garden, we began to look around for the neighbours who would be our friends and acquaintances from now on.

The manor stood on a great triangle of land, bounded by the river, the railway and the road. At one end of the road was the market-town of Ashford, at the other our village. So far, our hurried errands out of the house had all been to Ashford, where we picked up any food we needed along with the daily load of whitewash. But we had come down into Kent for country life, and now we began to turn our eyes in the direction of the village.

Howard warned us against it solemnly.

"You don't want to have nothing to do with them, whatever you do. I wouldn't want to tell you what I know about them," he said.

He was so earnest that we were shaken.

"Rubbish," said Timmy. "Probably they only gave the Colonel's scarlet runners second prize at the flower-show the year of the Boer War. I'm going to see what the pub's like anyway."

The vicar came to call.

"I'm afraid you'll find the parishioners an undesirable collection on the whole," he said. "It's a queer parish, very. I only took it because the last man didn't like flying bombs and asked me to exchange. But since I've come here, I've wondered if he was deceiving me and that it wasn't the flying bombs he minded. I should advise you very strongly to steer clear of the policeman. He's a very queer chap indeed. However, I expect the authorities will find him out before long."

We promised to go to church on Sunday and to steer clear of the policeman at all times.

The policeman came to call. He was young and extremely handsome and rather public-school.

"Natives are a rum lot," he said. "I've had to set the young chaps on slave-labour, building themselves a club, to get the place under control. Remind me to show you over sometime. My house is next-door to the pub. Only reason I took the job."

We went to the pub, looking nervously for signs of the Black Mass or Communist cells. There was the bristling hostility proper towards newcomers in the country, but nothing more. A sad little man with an Aldershot accent came in, drank up the week's supply of gin which had just been delivered and disappeared again, with a promise to return at the same time next week. The landlady, who was the only person to speak to us, described the beauty of her married daughter who lived in Rochester. We persevered, sitting meekly smiling towards the shove-ha'penny players, for a week, and at the end of that time were unenthusiastically invited to join in a game.

There was nothing to suggest the kind of secret life we were picturing. On the other hand they were more hostile than could be accounted for by our newness alone. Eventually we tracked it down to the fact that they objected to our sending Jane to the village school. They thought it was queer to live in the manor and do that, and they didn't like it. Possibly they were inarticulate idealists who felt that money should be spent first on education and only second on living conditions. But we never really got accepted there until Jane finished at the village school and went to the High School in Ashford.

We began to look around the neighbourhood for people who were not ruled by this particular prejudice. Callers began to call, and leave cards with Biddy, who put them in her apron-pockets and used them for writing lists of things she required from Ashford. We remembered that when we were married way back before the war, when calling was not so bizarre, we had been given a card-tray as a wedding present. We put it on the entailed table in the hall and presently it bloomed with Brigadiers and Admirals and Honourables.

"You know what?" said Timmy. "You ought to return those calls."

"I can't. I haven't got any engraved cards."

"You could say to the butlers that you're having some done with your new address but they haven't arrived yet."

"No, I couldn't, because there aren't any butlers. They all answer the door themselves. And scrub the doorstep. Howard said so."

The others were, as they knew, safe from being roped in for calling duty themselves because they all worked in the afternoon. I worked, as I pointed out when the subject was next raised, from six o'clock in the morning when I fed the baby, until midnight when I went round locking up the manor and switching off lights. As a matter of fact I was much harder-worked now than I had been even during the sixth year of the war. The only thing that kept me going was the beauty of my surroundings. You get a new fount of energy which is astonishing even to yourself, when you are in the grip of a new happiness. I have noticed it each time I had a new baby. By a thoughtful arrangement of nature, the newness of the baby doesn't wear off until it has begun to be slightly less slave-driving to its parent. Just now, it was the manor which kept my head above water and enabled me to get cheerfully Through my hundred-and-twenty-six-hour week. It wasn't so much the flowering trees beyond the open windows, and the continuous-performance bird-songs as the solid beauty of the things I worked with. Every cupboard-door was of thick, heavy, seasoned wood which fitted as though by air-pressure. Every cupboard had deep shelves, also of thick, hand-polished wood. Nothing ever jammed; nothing ever cracked; no handles ever came off; no keys jibbed at turning. The builders of this solid, unpretentious home had thought that these things mattered, because they thought that everyday domestic jobs mattered. Nothing was skimped or carelessly finished. Even the shelves in the housemaid's pantry were gracefully curved off at their ends. There is nothing more soothing, to a housewife, than being conscious, every moment of the day, that the workmen who prepared for her believed that her work rated the very best material. Also, when you have more space than you ever dreamed of, the wheels are oiled. There was a separate room for each task. The most welcome one of all was the Flower-Room, whose only purpose in life was for arranging the table flowers. It had a basin with taps, rows of shelves for vases, hooks on which to hang raffia and wire and a tiled floor. Doing the flowers was the best job of all, and it was wonderful not to be hurried over it, but to leave my materials scattered about when I broke off, as an artist leaves a half-finished creation, certain that no one will dare to tidy up his studio.

"But if you encouraged callers and cultivated the local gentry you'd have someone to admire your flower arrangements," coaxed Diana, when I had again firmly stood out against returning calls because I wanted to do the flowers instead. Diana was rather hankering after some high-flown social life, because the young sons of neighbouring manors were beginning to come back from the services, their pocket-books bulging with gratuities.

"I do the flowers for my own benefit," I said irritably, trying the arrangement of Howard's black sweet-peas in the centre of a rose-bowl, with scarlet next to them, then coral, then deep-pink, then light-pink, and the outer circle milky-pale, like mother-of-pearl. Then I put them all back in the basin and tried out the whole scheme beginning with the black and shading off through purple and mauve to the palest blue.

"It's ridiculous, taking all this trouble to make the manor look nice and then living in it like recluses," said Diana petulantly.

A large and splendid car swept in at the drive gates. But it went on past our door and down to Howard's cottage.

"The Colonel's daughter dropped in to see me," said Howard next day.

"I didn't know he had one."

"She was always a disappointment on account of the entail," admitted Howard. "But she's bought herself a place of her own in the next village now."

"I should have thought it was too painful to her to call at the manor," I remarked. I couldn't imagine what it would be like, if you had been brought up in it, to see it in the hands of strangers. Even now, in the first summer of my residence, I was ready to bristle up at the thought of anyone else ever living here.

"She came to mention something to me," said Howard. "It seems there's been a bit of a misunderstanding. I told you that agent doesn't know nothing. It seems that the refrigerator in the kitchen didn't belong to the house at all. The Colonel gave it to her before he died, and now she wants it back."

"You remember we said we weren't going to have any of those sordid disputes about things in the house once we lived in the manor," I said to the others later. "I'm sure if she says the refrigerator is really hers, it must be. People like her, brought up in a house like this, don't try to twist you the way our landlady did whose husband was doing time."

The refrigerator disappeared and we kept milk on the slate slabs in the larder.

"Those fire extinguishers," said Howard, a few days later. "She couldn't understand why they'd been left for you. It seems she had some arrangement with the Colonel about them."

"Then of course she must have them," I agreed. The fire-extinguishers disappeared.

"The Colonel's daughter is just moving into her new house," said Howard chattily, as he brought in an immense basket of black-currants. "She dropped in to ask me if I'd stored the linoleum for her that she wants to put on the bathroom floors there."

"And had you?"

"Well, it's still down along your back passage," said Howard.

"Tell her to come and make an afternoon call and roll it up and take it away with her then," said Diana, who was setting out the bottling-jars for the currants.

"Don't say nothing, but she doesn't mean to call," said Howard.

"Those Cox's apple-trees in the orchard," said Howard.

"The ones you said were the best trees in the garden?"

"Yes. Well, I didn't say nothing about it, but the Colonel planted those the night his daughter was born."

"He seems to have had some strange habits."

"There's not many like him," said Howard. "And you see, she feels as a matter of respect she ought not to leave them to strangers."

"Any night she cares to come and dig them up again and take them away under her arm will be all right with us."

For some weeks I used to look apprehensively towards the Coxes, when I put the baby under the trees for his morning sleep, but they were still there. Once, in an outhouse, I found a little chair and nursery table and some old-fashioned toys tied up together in a bundle.

"She sold them when the house was empty," said Howard. "Someone gave her four-and-six for the lot, but they never called to fetch them."

When Howard saw us all dressed for church, he said we must be sure to sit in the manor pew.

"Not for a moment," we said firmly. "It would look as if we were setting up to be squire."

"That it wouldn't," said Howard. "The Colonel got converted." He added that since his forefathers had all filled the village church with windows and tablets and tombstones, everyone had prophesied that when he became a Roman Catholic he would have to pay for it, and that no one was at all surprised when the family died out with his daughter.

We sat modestly in the back pew, leaving the manor one, with its own door, as empty as it had been since the Colonel's defection. We knew Howard couldn't find out because of not being on speaking terms with anyone in the village. Timmy read the first lesson, in his deep and beautiful broadcasting voice, well known in a million homes. Lefty barked his way through the second, as though he was giving a particularly dumb bunch of landlubbers their first lesson in seamanship during a dangerous storm.

The children behaved beautifully and a kind of peace stole over us all. It was good to get up early on Sunday, instead of wandering about in dressing-gowns and having Brunch. It was good to know that the children were headed for the best kind of English childhood, with its routine of hair-washing before the nursery fire on Saturday night, and clean clothes next morning, and sitting still in church and going home to roast-beef and gooseberry tart at one prompt.

We watched the villagers stream out and the parson shook hands with us.

"Both lessons were all right but of course the second immeasurably better read than the first," he said.

The congregation was hanging round the gate to watch us go out. There was one man in very expensive tweeds, very new. We recognized him as a famous dress designer.

"Oh, my *dear*," he said loudly to his companion as we came up. "*Did* you see the *raffish* B.B.C. crowd in the back pew? I thought *any* moment they were going to break into a song and dance, didn't you?"

Jane was the only one who made any headway with our neighbours. At her previous school she had consorted with the children of the Yugoslav embassy and various dispossessed royalty.

"How do you like the village school?" we asked her.

"*Much* nicer. They're not nearly so rough," she said.

The head teacher called to ask us if I would stop Jane drinking other children's allocation of free school milk as well as her own. "I don't *want* it," she said. "But the boys are so hurt if I don't. I hate milk anyway."

It turned out that she had been adopted as the Primary Pin-Up-Girl and there was passionate competition to stand her drinks. When we got this tidied up, the farmers' sons soon started giving her rides on their ponies and she came home grumbling that she was under-privileged because she hadn't got one of her own.

"The Colonel was just the same," said Howard, listening sympathetically. "After he put down his hunters, he couldn't bear to go near the stable."

On Saturday morning Jane said she had an errand in Ashford and went off with her pocket-money. On Friday, when the *Kentish Express* came out, I was surprised to see two or three men leading ponies up the drive.

"It's the address it gave in the advertisement," they protested.

All day the ponies kept on coming. When Jane came home from school she wept to see them turned away.

"She ought to have a pony, you know," said Howard, coming back from turning a truculent gipsy and his ragged animal off the premises. He and Jane saw eye to eye about little girls being owed ponies as a natural law. He carried on only an intermittent feud with the farmer across the fields and one day, when it was in the intermission, he went over and invited the farmer's pony to stay for the week-end. From then on it was a regular visitor. We asked Howard if there was anything we could do in return for the farmer. "Don't say nothing, but he keeps all his stuff in your shed as it is," Howard said. We went to look in the shed beyond the large woodshed, down by the river, and sure enough it was full of harrows, tractors, hay-carts and bits of harvester. It explained a constant coming and going which we had noticed on the back drive, but had dismissed, vaguely, as being visitors to Howard's cottage. Now we began to notice it, we had a whole set of companions around the place. There was a man who kept his motor-cycle at the back of the cow-shed and called twice a day to park it and fetch it again. We never discovered who he was. The keeper from a big estate, who liked dead chickens to give his ferrets, could often be seen leaning speculatively over the hen-yard gate, noting if any of them were looking off colour. There were some men who used to tell me where the hens were laying away, in the long grass by the river. Howard said they were platelayers on the railway line and the man from the signal-box. They had a traditional right to get water from our stable-tap, and they seemed to need quite a lot.

One day, there were three men standing knee-deep in the river. They wished me good-morning as I went by. Later on I found them cutting down a tree and thought this was pressing hospitality too far.

"There's nothing you can do," said Howard when I found him. "They got a right to do anything at all they like. They're the Kent Catchment Board. You say a word to them and they'll get up all the mud out of the river and spread it over the garden so that nothing will grow that year at all. You can't stop them. You just leave them to me. Most times I can manage to keep them in hand, but if you was to annoy them there's no saying what they might do."

Every day a man in a bowler hat came out of the second cottage and walked up the drive without saying a word to us and walked back again, still speechless, at half-past five. Every Friday morning Howard brought in fifteen shillings and a rent-book for me to sign.

"Some day I've *got* to know who he is," I said to Howard as he put the book away in his apron-pocket.

"You just leave it to me and don't say nothing," said Howard. "I told that agent I'd get it all fixed up for you."

We didn't need the cottage. We already had far more room than we could use, and the fifteen shillings was quite useful. Also, no one could possibly have been less trouble than the bowler-hatted one. When we learned that a neighbouring manor, the other side of the village, had been requisitioned and was steadily ruined, we began to comprehend that Howard had defended his manor by a series of complicated plots and that the price of victory had been giving up one cottage to the government. If the bowler hat discovered from us that we still had eight or nine empty rooms, he might bring eight or nine fellow-employees to move in. This was the nightmare of Howard's life, and we began to subscribe to it and hide behind the beech hedge when we saw our tenant approaching.

I couldn't understand why the others still sighed about being lonely, and said it was like being enemy soldiers in an occupied country, because, from my own particular little rut, the day seemed full of company and I wanted no other. There were weeks when I didn't set foot outside the drive gates. I telephoned my shopping orders twice a week, and the carrier delivered them. The baker and butcher and fishmonger called, and I chose the goods from their vans. The day fell into patches of well-worn routine; beginning with the fruit and vegetables coming in and the hens' hot mash going out; progressing through tradesmen's cups of tea to the gardeners' mid-morning cocoa; to Colin's rest in the garden and the baby's liberation on to the lawns, up to the arrival in the kitchen of the day's eggs, which was the last job the boy did before he went home. There was always something happening. Gooseberries would swell and ripen suddenly and have to be bottled at once, or the boy would chop his finger in the garden or someone come dashing in to use our telephone because a passing train had set fire to the cornfield. Tramps arrived and had to be given food and drink because they always had been. Village children were sent to ask for the usual flowers for school festivities and the verger for red roses for the church at Whitsun. It was a peaceful, orderly and utterly absorbing routine and I didn't want it interrupted from outside. If I saw callers at the gate, I disappeared right down to the bottom of the garden by the river gate. I didn't want to sit and make conversation in the drawing-room. I wanted to get the old manor recipe for artichoke soup from Howard's old wife and get Biddy to try it, and catch the farmer to ask for some hay for the pony and consult with Howard about trying a new spot for the strawberry-bed. At night, when the others came home, their talk of London seemed far away and meaningless.

Colin, who was four, came into the heritage of freedom which he had been denied all the years he had been made to keep within call in case of daylight air-raids or flying bombs. He attached himself to Howard and the boy so that I hardly saw him indoors. When I looked out of my window at dawn, I would see him running across the grass, with the dew wet on his sandals, off on some mysterious errand of his own among the trees. At midday, he sat in the woodshed, in the dusky half-light among the smell of sawn logs, sharing the gardeners' cocoa and bread and cheese. Howard showed him how to wring a chicken's neck and how to trap field-mice among the peas and to kill snakes in the long grass. He showed him how to plant peas, and water flowers when the sun was off them, and where the chaffinch had a nest with eggs in it, and how to use a bill-hook on nettles and build a hen-house out of old pieces of wood. It was his right—not a patronizing indulgence—to ride back from the rubbish-heap in the empty wheelbarrow. It was his right to be driven in the tradesmen's vans up the back drive and along the road to the front gate and be put down there, just as the smallest new tomato in the greenhouse and the pullet's first small egg were his by long tradition. He grew unbelievably handy with a rake and a saw, and would not even look up if anyone came into the woodshed while he was watching Howard shape planks and whittle an axle for a new wheelbarrow. Every boy should have a year at the heels of an old craftsman sometime in his life. A dozen nursery schools could not have given Colin the half of what Howard gave him. Howard accepted him, with serious and conscientious calm, like a schoolmaster who has got countless generations of boys through their first Latin primer and then let them go, satisfied that the foundations have been well laid.

"That boy ought to have a dog, you know," he said. "He needs one at his age."

"So he ought," I said. "Where can we get one?"

"Don't say nothing to him and I'll see him right," said Howard. He went to the market next Tuesday and came home with a likely-looking golden retriever puppy. The puppy, which we named Doubtful, and Colin immediately settled down with each other, and Colin's life was complete. Once I asked him if he could remember our old house in the suburbs.

"Did we have another house?" he asked without interest, and departed to his man's world among the outbuildings. I only saw him in the evenings and on Sundays.

Up in the village, where I never went now, the boys had finished building their Youth Club. The policeman called to ask if my husband could get some famous character to open it ceremonially. He suggested Tommy Handley.

Our stock went up in the village like a rocket. When I went into the town to get Colin's hair cut, all the women on the village bus wished me good-day. I was bewildered, because I had quite settled down to sulky stares and whispered conversations, with glances in my direction and didn't mind them at all now. People stopped us after church. When the dog Doubtful ran off to the village, he was sent back, with a string attached to his collar and a polite message, carried by willing children. At the pub, Timmy and Lefty and Bob and my husband were stood drinks every night and invited to compete for a place in the shove-ha'penny team. Radio stars were, as a matter of business, ten a penny in our lives and it had never occurred to us that they could have any bearing on our standing in the country. No one had ever heard of Diana or any play she was in, or any of her famous friends. But radio stars, we realized now, belonged in every cottage and every council-house kitchen.

The prestige spread to Ashford. The villagers told us that both the *Kentish Express* and the *Kent Messenger* were going to send reporters to the ceremony. When one of the national Sunday papers featured the Youth Club and Tommy Handley's coming visit on the front page, they gathered in the village street to watch us come back from church. We had a nervous idea that they would break out any moment into "God Bless the Old Squire".

The Youth Club was decorated with garlands. All week, the mothers of club members baked cakes with their own rations for the festive tea. Women called at our house to borrow tablecloths and consult about hiring a tea-urn.

On the Saturday morning, Timmy and Diana went to meet Tommy's train. I had a faint, unspoken uneasiness all morning, because I knew that radio stars are apt to be vague about personal appearances undertaken, in an expansive moment, for friendship's sake and repented of afterwards. I comforted myself by remembering that Tommy's reputation in this way was unusually good.

The taxi came back containing Timmy and Diana alone.

"He wasn't on the train," they said. "And there isn't another. We asked."

Already the news-reel men were setting up their cameras in the lane, and children in their best clothes taking up positions all along it. Some of the club boys came in the drive gate, in their Sunday suits, to escort Tommy down after lunch. Biddy had just put the cold chicken on the table and was hanging about ready to catch a glimpse of the great man.

I went to hide in the attic, hot with shame and embarrassment. I cursed the moment we had agreed to take any interest in the village at all. We had been perfectly happy before, ignored and ignoring. But now—I couldn't see how we could go on living in the district any longer. Then the telephone rang.

"I thought you got into Kent from Victoria," said Tommy's voice.

"Not our part of Kent. It's from Charing Cross."

"I'm at Victoria, and they say there isn't a train," said Tommy, and rang off. But I knew he would come, because he was an old trouper and looked upon trains as the natural enemies of his profession and made a point of getting to his destination in spite of them. Sure enough he turned up in a hired car from Maidstone an hour or so later, and was greeted all the more enthusiastically because of the suspense. The news-reel cameras whirred and the local boys poked their heads in front of them to be in the picture with Tommy. The local reporters never stopped scribbling in their note-books. The parson and the policeman were seen to give each other a curt nod across the tea-table. Tommy signed autographs and made believe to lose the ceremonial key at the crucial moment and borrowed the policeman's helmet and wore it and the boys from the primary school fought brutally for the chairs at either side of Jane. The famous dress designer leered in the background; neighbouring parsons dropped in, smiling benignly and there was a thick sprinkling of the callers to whom I owed visiting cards.

One rather terrifying woman in tweeds kept on appearing close to us and then joining in the melee to get near Tommy. Just at the end, as Tommy, exhausted, was fighting his way to the door, with Lefty and Bob as bodyguard, the vicar tapped me on the shoulder. "There's a lady here *very* anxious to be introduced to you," he murmured. But I was swept away from him in the crush.

"The Colonel's daughter came over specially to that youth club tea," said Howard next day. "She wanted to meet Tommy Handley. Didn't you see her there?"

We really and truly had arrived at last.

4

THERE came a time when even the buckets of flowers left ready twice a week in the flower-room could not console me for the slavery of my life. From dawn till midnight I was running—along the corridors, through the dining-hall, down the front-stairs and up the back. It started when I ran to the kitchen, before anyone was up, for the baby's first feed. If I forgot the sugar, I had to cover the course again. By the time I reached the thirty-third room with my broom and mop, the first one had gathered a complete new coating of dust. It was like painting the Forth Bridge, which (so the story runs) requires a new coat at the beginning by the time the painters have reached the end.

"Look here," said Timmy. "Didn't we plan that we would always have orderly meals and clean sheets and friends to stay for the week-end when we got our country manor? Half the time we're eating snacks on a tray just like we used to in the war."

I asked Howard if there was any woman in the village who would help.

"There's not one of them would set foot in the place. They all know how big it is. I tried to get one for you that's not quite right in the head, but she won't come either."

Biddy, who was getting sulky on account of the work, said there was a girl in her native village back in Ireland who wanted to see the world. When I filled in the various permits I discovered she was only sixteen.

"It's going to be like having another child to look after," I said. "We shan't be able to let her out alone."

After several false alarms, and by the time we had entirely given up the idea, Maureen turned up unexpectedly one night. She was blonde, undersized and skinny and weeping with fatigue. When she handed me her ration-book I realized from its colour that she had lied about her age and was fourteen.

"She looks and talks as if she was the same age as Jane. It's ridiculous," I grumbled.

Maureen was not interested in housework but she discovered my typewriter and took it to the kitchen and wrote poetry on it with one finger while Biddy cooked and washed up. I was worried about how she should spend her afternoon off. Biddy passed it on to me that she wanted to have her wages instantly and go to a real hairdresser. She came back with her hair cut in the most extraordinary jagged edges and in floods of tears.

"They wouldn't perm it," she sobbed.

Biddy stood behind her, absent-mindedly making dabs at the hair and cracking what she found there between her finger and thumb. "I think I'll sweep the children's room myself in future, Maureen," I said nervously.

"Naturally she's not interested in her work," said Timmy, who had been drawn into making personal appearances at youth clubs, and regarded himself as an expert in adolescent mentality. "She never has any stimulating recreation or the company of people her own age. You must find her some congenial spare-time activity."

Maureen turned down the Girls' Friendly without waiting for me to explain what it was, but agreed to go to the weekly dance at the Youth Club which Tommy Handley had opened.

"I don't know if we ought to let her loose among those great lads," I fretted. "Some of them are seventeen or so. They may have ideas."

"I'll get the best of the club lads, which isn't saying much, to call for her and bring her home," said the policeman.

The pick of the Youth Club turned up on Saturday night and received our instructions about returning his partner at the side door by ten o'clock prompt. The Colonel's lady herself could not have picked a more suitable party to walk out with the house-parlourmaid. He was thick-set, rubicund and with such a witless expression that my husband said, as the door closed on them, "One thing you can be sure of, he can't have any ideas."

Maureen was very firm that she hadn't enjoyed the club dance, but all the same she went again next Saturday.

"That lad says he won't call for her again," the policeman told us.

"Wasn't she his type?" we asked, disappointed.

The policeman whistled and said, "Hot stuff."

Howard kept on saying that Maureen's little bedroom was damp. We had put her in the old butler's bedroom because it was a nice little square room near the kitchen, very cosy, with a parquet floor. We had painted it pink and dolled it up with spotted net curtains and pink bows.

"Don't say nothing about it to that agent, but that floor sweats," said Howard. "The Colonel kept bags of salt there and it's never been the same since."

"Why didn't he keep the butler there?" we wanted to know.

"You know why you have the butler sleeping by the back door?" asked Howard kindly. We didn't know.

"It's so that he can look out the maids' followers," Howard explained. "But the last butler took to letting in his own lady friends instead. If you get my meaning."

We got it and moved Maureen a very long way upstairs, next to Diana. Maureen cried a lot and said she was afraid to sleep there. When we asked why, she said they had told her in the village that it was haunted. The Colonel walked up and down it at night because he had never approved of the way the New Wing was built. When we told Howard he was really angry for the first time.

"The Colonel was as nice an old gentleman as you could wish to meet. She's no need to be afraid of *him*," he said stiffly.

We got Maureen a dark-blue dress and a little frilly apron. With her straggly blonde hair and skinny little knees she looked like something out of a variety show in a C company touring the sticks. We asked Peter and Ann, who lived in a little flat in London, down for the week-end. By noon on Saturday they had decided they couldn't live a minute longer without a Kentish manor of their own. They knocked up the estate agent on Saturday afternoon and took us all round the countryside in their car. There were a lot of Kent's great houses going begging that year. No one would take on anything big because the memory of fuel shortages and no domestic help was still too fresh. We saw a moated grange and a Queen Ann rectory and a Georgian manor on the outskirts of Tenterden. But nothing we saw was in the same class as our own enchanting house.

At dinner on Saturday evening we had asparagus and French beans and new potatoes and raspberries, all straight from the garden, and two roast pullets straight from the hen-yard. We drank Kentish cider out of a cask.

"Oh, you *are* lucky," Peter and Ann kept on saying. We answered severely that we had earned it all by the sweat of our brows. We sat by the open French windows in the drawing-room and the smell of the night-scented stock which Howard had planted for us wafted up and mingled with the scent of the coffee Maureen was handing round before she went off to her Saturday night's innocent fun. We sat there for a long time. It was so still that you could hear every little scuffling of creatures in the shrubbery and when an owl cried it hit us like the last trump.

Now that we had Maureen, we had people to stay every week-end. Every Friday morning I went into the kitchen and Biddy got a pencil and paper and we worked out menus for the week-end. Howard looked as if he had suddenly been restored to a world from which he had been long exiled. He went around the garden with a furrowed brow, calculating what would be ready for each week-end. All the Londoners adored him. They would hang around the cold frames listening to him talk for hours on end. Peter and Ann were peevish because they couldn't find a manor with a quaint old gardener of their own. On Friday afternoons, he brought in garden-baskets full of food and buckets full of flowers and on Friday evening the station taxi brought its new load of admiring visitors. It was lovely, being able to share all the things everyone was pining for that year—the candlelit table with its glowing roses, and Sunday morning with its dawn chorus and village church bells, and Jane's pony courteously accepting bits of apple and tea under the may-tree on Sunday afternoons. Even Biddy cheered up, because everyone was so overwhelmed by the atmosphere that all the guests felt obliged to tip her more than they could afford.

One Saturday evening, Diana said, with her eyes on the ceiling, "Why is Maureen walking across my room?"

I explained that she went up while we were eating to put her things ready for the village dance.

"I still don't see why she need go through my room to get to hers," said Diana.

I was in the frame of mind of an amateur mechanic who has at last succeeded in getting a car to tick over, after hours of hopeless labour, and could not face anything going wrong with the domestic situation now. I privately thought that if Maureen was borrowing a little of Diana's make-up to impress the Club boys, it would be all the same in a hundred years, because Diana had far more than she ever used.

Biddy's husband was demobbed and came home richer than anyone in the house. He got bored while Biddy was doing the chores and drifted off to market and came home with a dozen of the most unattractive hens I ever saw, and put them in the disused pig-sty. Howard refused to feed them. Times had changed, he admitted readily. He was willing to face the fact that the Reds were sweeping the country and the old Colonel doubtless whirling like a teetotum in his grave. But still he drew the line at ministering to the hens of the cook's husband.

"Don't say nothing to that fellow, but it's my opinion they've got the fowl-pest," he said.

Biddy's husband spent hours leaning on the pig-sty gate and watching them, but could not remember to feed them. I was driven to doing it myself. I pointed out her wifely duty to Biddy, but she said she wasn't speaking to her husband at the moment.

It struck me one Monday morning, when I sent Maureen up to collect a glass which Diana had left in her bedroom, that you could not, in fact, hear her, when she did walk across Diana's room. But next Saturday evening there was the same clop-clop of footsteps at the same time.

One afternoon next week I couldn't find my red coat to go up to the village post-office.

"I suppose I didn't by any chance leave it in the kitchen?" I asked Biddy, who was sitting there sombrely knitting.

"You'd better ask Maureen," she said.

"Where is Maureen?"

"Gone out with a G.I."

"I didn't know she knew any G.I.'s."

Biddy gave a short sarcastic laugh. I went out to the drive gate to look for Maureen. Howard was scything nettles in the orchard.

"Don't say nothing now," I said, "But did you see Maureen go out?"

"Yes, I did, Madam," said Howard with immense significance.

"What was she wearing?"

"A red coat."

"She hasn't got a red coat."

"Ah," said Howard. "I could have told you a thing or two about that girl, but I didn't want to say nothing to anybody."

In the village I asked Catherine Garton, who also went to the Youth Club dances, what sort of clothes Maureen wore to them. She gave me an exact description of Diana's wardrobe, including the high-heeled shoes. They accounted for the clop-clop of footsteps which Maureen did not make in her own little shoes. Diana's must have been several sizes too big. But what I did not understand, and never shall, is how Diana could have taken her coffee-cup, week after week, without noticing the donor was wearing her shoes.

"Sorry for the mess it puts you in, but at least the mothers of my club boys will let them come back to the club now," said the policeman kindly, meeting me in the street.

Biddy was smug. She acted exactly as if Maureen had been my over-indulged daughter of whom I was now rightly ashamed. "I wouldn't have said anything," she said. "But every time I come in the kitchen I catch her on my husband's knee. He was a good man as you could wish to see, until he met her."

"Fourteen years old," I reflected, despairingly.

"She's been no better than she should be since she was eleven," said Biddy. "That was the year the G.I.'s moved into our village. After they moved out she wanted a job in England so as to go after them. That's why she came."

I locked the doors so that Maureen would have to ring when she came in. When I opened the door, she shot off into the darkness. I followed her and collected the red coat off Howard's wheelbarrow where she had dumped it. The G.I. stood on the doorstep, watching us in some confusion.

Maureen's room was such a litter of other people's possessions that after a time I couldn't sort out which were my own. Maureen wept monotonously.

"Mam, is your husband in?" asked the G.I.

"He's having his supper."

"Mam, I want to speak to him in private."

They were in the study for a long time and came out looking sober. My husband solemnly beckoned me in and closed the door.

"See here," he said to me, "Why don't you give this kid a break?"

"I don't know what you're talking about," I said.

"See here," he said. "This kid's a good kid. But she's never had a break. People like us, on the up-and-up, got no right to give her the run-a-round like this. She needs a chance to make good, same as we needed one ourselves once."

I put the point of view to Biddy, but she invited me to choose between Maureen and herself.

I took Maureen up to London, to the most aristocratic agency I could find, and requested them to find some philanthropists who thought they could combine reform with light domestic labour. "If you'll just let me ring up the top of my waiting-list," said the manageress, thumbing through a schedule about the same length as the telephone directory.

Twenty minutes later, Maureen was installed in a luxury flat, with her own radio and private bathroom and the most earnest promises that she should never be asked to do more than a few ladylike tasks. The family, crowding round her fondly, asked her merely to name any little amenity she fancied.

I never saw her again. But the thing which puzzled me most was that she and Biddy used to have the most affectionate and friendly telephone conversations, on a trunk line, most days in the week. I didn't discover until long afterwards that Maureen was reversing the charges.

"Why don't you try that girl Catherine?" said the policeman. "Her family only moved to the village recently so she hasn't had time to get like the rest of them yet."

Outside a stained-glass window, I never saw a more saintly-looking girl. She had blue eyes, a white forehead, thick wavy hair and a very sweet smile. It was a pleasure just to sit and look at her. "I don't want a girl anything like Maureen again," I said to her, feeling apologetic for mentioning it.

"Madam," said Catherine. "At the village where I came from we had Americans. Every single girl in the village had a baby by a G.I. All except me. You ask anyone."

I asked the policeman, who said it was perfectly true. We all felt quite overawed when Catherine moved in. We had no hesitation at all about putting her in the little pink room which had been the butler's bedroom. If we had a passing qualm it was that the decor should have been pure white instead.

Peter and Ann brought a millionaire to stay.

"He's my best account," said Peter, who was in advertising. "I'd hoped that Ann and I would have found a place of our own by the time he came over. You *will* tell us first if ever you decide to give up the manor, won't you?"

We smiled patronizingly and agreed to entertain the millionaire.

"He's set his heart on seeing a real, old-fashioned country house week-end, like the ones he's heard about," said Peter. "Just charge anything you spend up to me and I'll charge it up to expenses."

I don't think there was a single soul on the manor (apart from Biddy) who actually hoped to get any share of the million dollars. But there was a mounting sense of excitement as his visit approached. Millionaires are, after all, not just rich men. They are a species. They are rather like the Romans and Gauls of one's Batin exercise book. They are forever turning up in stories and films and newspapers, but you hardly expect to see one in real life. Howard cut the few bunches of small, sourish grapes off our outdoor vine, and brought in the peaches off the south wall and arranged them on fig-leaves on a plate himself.

There was much, discussion as to who should be asked to make up the party. My old father, who was a parson, settled half the problem by turning up unexpectedly and installing himself in a steamy little room above the kitchen, which we called Little Hell and which he loved because he could smell the bacon frying as he dressed. Peter telephoned to say he didn't want to be a nuisance, but if we could find a title to complete the party he thought he'd be able to ask the millionaire to transfer another of his company's accounts to the agency as well.

Bob had been in the R.A.F., in Cairo, with an earl's daughter who was in the W.A.A.F.s.

"Do you really think she'd like our sort of week-end?" we asked doubtfully. Bob explained the whole thing to her, including Peter's account. She was quite willing to do a good turn to an old comrade-in-arms and undertook to think up ideas about how an American millionaire would expect an English lady to behave on an old-fashioned country-house week-end party, by Friday.

On Friday evening I lit the log fire in the hall. It danced merrily over the expanse of white walls and black wood. It looked like the opening of a costume drama.

"Give me a good Triplex grate with coal in it," said my father. "I often wonder why you didn't take a nice little house in the suburbs. You could have paid for half of it by now on a good mortgage."

The millionaire was terribly nervous. None of us could get him to talk. After dinner, in the drawing-room we had some draught cider before we went to bed. He kept on picking up his glass and then putting it down again untouched. At last he beckoned Peter out of the room and said we ought not to be drinking liquor with the sky-pilot there. He went to bed early.

The Magnolia Room had glowing chrysanthemums in it, and my grandmother's linen coverlet spread on the bed, but its mirror was one of our less successful bargains. When we had got it home from the junk-shop we had found that it belonged to the pre-quicksilver era. The millionaire arrived down to breakfast with his chin festooned with cotton-wool.

"I cut myself a bit shaving," he said.

His hand shook so that he could hardly get a cigarette out of his gold cigarette-case. He had a gold lighter but no flame. My father, who shaved himself all his life with an old-fashioned cut-throat, so sharp that one quiver of the wrist meant suicide, watched him in fascinated horror. At last he could bear it no longer and snapped on his Utility lighter, which always lit at the first flick and held the shaking cigarette still enough to light.

"Look here, you can get one of these for four-and-six. I'll show you the shop," he said firmly.

On the Sunday, Peter hired two cars from the local firm to take us all to service in Canterbury Cathedral. The Red Dean preached. The millionaire, as he listened, got more and more nervous. My father got steadily gloomier. The earl's daughter, a Roman Catholic, supposed that this was a typical Anglican service and listened with polite attention.

On the way back from Canterbury one of the cars broke down. We picked blackberries from the hedges to soothe the pangs of hunger. "I often wonder why you don't stick to that nice little village church of yours just up the road," said my father.

We got home at three o'clock. Biddy and Catherine had kept lunch hot for us.

"I do hope you won't mind, Madam," said Catherine. "But my boy called in unexpectedly, just to say good-bye. He's been ordered to the Far East. I didn't take any time from doing the table."

The evening seemed endless. Next morning, when the house was blissfully empty again, I decided that we would never try to put on a show week-end again. It was altogether too much of a strain. "I'm sorry about the week-end, Peter," I said when he telephoned later in the week.

"I don't know what you mean," said Peter. "He's never stopped talking about it since. He says it's just what he expected. He's always heard these high-class house parties were a bit on the formal side."

We never saw the millionaire again, but he has sent us a Christmas card of his country house in Connecticut every year since. Also, he and my father kept up a regular correspondence for the rest of my father's life. I often wonder what on earth the letters can have been about.

5

ONE Sunday after lunch we had to wait a long time for our coffee.

At last the door opened and Biddy's face looked in instead of Catherine's. I followed her into the hall.

"Catherine's trying to kill me," she said.

"What with?"

"The carving-knife."

"At least you could bring the coffee with you, I should have thought."

I went back into the drawing-room and asked for suggestions.

"Why does everything have to happen to us?" my husband said irritably. I was beginning to realize, dimly, that it was because we were trying to live in a way that didn't suit our own bit of history. It was like adding screws that didn't fit to a machine. Once you do that, not only does the machine refuse to work, but all sorts of apparently unconnected accidents happen.

Lefty and Bob went off to take the carving-knife away, but came back to say that Biddy's husband had already done so. He was a Commando.

"What started it, anyway?" I asked Biddy, who was sitting in the kitchen looking indignant and paying no attention to the coffee. She said it was a radio programme.

"Which one?"

She thumbed through the *Radio Times* and said it was called, "To Start You Talking." The announcer had asked if it was right for girls with fiancés in the Far East to go out dancing with other men.

"Yes, but what then?" I asked.

Biddy said she had turned it off after Catherine had leaped across the table with a carving-knife and been snatched back just as the knife touched her throat, so hadn't listened to the rest. I went out to the pig-sty and asked Biddy's husband for his version.

"I wouldn't know what it was about," he said, watching his bedraggled hens.

Catherine had locked herself in the butler's bedroom and refused to answer.

"It's a case for the police," said Lefty, who likes jobs to be devolved to the proper authority, since his time in the Navy.

I borrowed his bicycle and went up to the police-station and the policeman bicycled back with me. Catherine, who seemed gratified at learning that he had been called in, opened her door when he announced himself.

"You know what nearly happened to you, Catherine?" he said. "You were nearly taken into a mortuary to view Biddy laid out on a cold slab, like those slabs in the larder there." I was immensely impressed by his approach, which I could certainly never have thought of myself, but which had an astonishing effect on Catherine, who stopped looking pleased with herself and turned white and burst into tears. As his description progressed I began to feel squeamish myself and went to join the others picking pears on the back drive. The policeman cycled by, remarking casually, "She won't do it again."

I wasn't as surprised as I might have been when Catherine's mother called to see me. She was a thin, sad, bedraggled little woman about half Catherine's size. But by her side was a tall, handsome boy, well dressed and with a haughty, morose expression.

There exists a particular routine patter, as I learned during my time at the manor, for breaking the news of an illegitimate baby—or rather two distinct routines, one old and one new.

The older generation—particularly those once in "good service" make a long tale of it, starting with a warning gloom of approach, progressing through a kind of guessing-game ("Have you noticed anything about . . . ?") to tears and then, those dried, a discussion, pitched in a suitably minor key, about future plans. The post-war girls are brisker and never use the phrase "in trouble" or anything like it, but refer matter-of-factly to "the baby" and immediately go on to a financial discussion of ways and means, mostly about maternity grants and paternity allocations and three months off work on sick relief. Catherine's mother was, of course, one of the old-fashioned type of news-breaker. But she was also so fluent that I couldn't quite pick up my cues.

I hastily reviewed the blameless trips to the cinema which had been Catherine's only recreation since she came.

"Weren't you late back from church one Sunday?" asked the mother accusingly.

"Oh, yes—I believe we were."

"Well, you see," she said with deep reproach.

"I'm most terribly sorry," I found myself saying.

It was clearly expected that I should tidy up the disaster which my own inadequacy had caused. Catherine's mother, who had been, she said, employed in a house like the manor herself until she married, was perfectly clear that a domestic service employer took over all arrangements at this stage. But Catherine had been born into an age when the welfare organization was all set to cope with her dilemma. As a matter of fact, Catherine got the best of both worlds and was not unnaturally pleased with herself and her arrangements.

We wrote to the War Office, who courteously concerned themselves with the future status of Catherine's baby by sending out to the Far East to get his father to come home on compassionate leave to his wedding. The S.S.A.F.A. representative called regularly about baby-equipment and hospitals and wedding arrangements. Since both Reg, the boy, and Catherine were still in their teens, all sons of consents had to be obtained and forms filled in, so that I was continually in and out of the miserable tied cottage where Catherine's family lived. You crossed a sea of stinking mud to get to it, and it consisted of one living-room, with no ceiling, but the roof-angle as plain from inside as from outside, and with brick walls with no plaster on them. The family slept in two wretched little cupboards opening off it. It was incredible that the tall, beautiful and well-groomed Catherine should have emerged from here. It was even more incredible that Catherine should be the joint production of the bedraggled, carefully humble little woman and her husband. He was a dwarfish, round-headed, speechless little man, worn into dumb stupidity by physical labour. They had five dwarfish and round-headed younger children. Only Catherine and the eldest boy were fair and tall with oval faces and straight, dark eyebrows like an Egyptian painting, and a haughty, arrogant way of carrying themselves.

"Where's your eldest son?" I asked once.

"Back at his boarding-school," said the mother, with some pride. The father muttered something about a gun.

"He tried to shoot the superintendent again so they stopped his half-holiday this week," the mother explained. I remember nervously that once when he called to see Catherine I had found him hanging round Lefty's gun-cupboard.

The more I saw of them, the more it struck me how much the machinery of the new welfare state turned for them, without making a ha'porth of difference to the way they chose to conduct their lives. The trigger-happy son was being educated at an establishment which (except for being comfortable) was exactly like a public-school. The Youth Employment Service had got their third child apprenticed to a cycle-factory and a bicycle to get there. Their M.P. was for ever pestering generals about their unborn grandchild. But they remained unsurprised, unchanged, serenely themselves.

The War Office got so fussed about Catherine's baby that they returned the bridegroom to England before we got the wedding fixed. He decided to stay for the week-end. One thing about the manor was that you could include any number of passing strangers under its hospitable roof and never even notice that they were there. But this time we were so full of the idea that Reg and Catherine were to be encouraged to go straight that we put Reg in the butler's bedroom and Catherine in Little Hell and locked the door of the New Wing to separate them and took the key away. My husband paused with the key in his hand to say:

"We ought to make sure Catherine's asleep in bed."

"We can't wake the poor child up for that."

But next morning I suddenly came wide awake at once, with a certain foreboding and went into Little Hell and found the bed empty and unslept in. I hesitated; then remembered the Colonel's lady, draped my dressing-gown more securely round me and marched down the back stairs. Biddy, who was making toast in the kitchen, looked at me sardonically. I banged on the door of the butler's bedroom.

"Come out, I know you're both in there," I called.

There was a long pause during which I felt remarkably foolish. It crossed my mind that the Colonel's lady would probably have donned her tweeds much earlier in the scene.

Reg and Catherine emerged, looking utterly amazed and not downcast at all. They stared up and down the corridor, perhaps expecting it to be on fire. They could not imagine why else they should have been so abruptly summoned from what they regarded as a legitimate marital chamber, now that all the forms had been signed. It was clear that the script called for a lecture from me, on some clear-cut moral issues, if we were to proceed any further. But their frank astonishment put me off my stride. Alas, Howard was just coming in the back door with a basket of brussels sprouts. I said I would speak to them later.

After a lot of priming from the others at breakfast I got up a reasonable pep talk. Catherine wept, but simply because her mother had taught her that it is the proper tribute to pay to the moral reflections of an employer. She overdid it, in my opinion, by sitting weeping in the kitchen all day, which meant I had to do her work. As I was exhaustedly combing my hair before Sunday supper (cold, not to keep the maids from any devotions they might plan, as Howard had explained to us) there was a knock at my bedroom door. Reg came in and dumped his kit on the floor. I stared at him in weary astonishment.

"I just wanted to thank you for having me. It's been a grand week-end," he said. He wasn't joking, either. We shook hands warmly and he departed.

Catherine was to be married from the home of Reg's aunt in Grimsby. It all seemed most dreadfully drab. Diana searched through her clothes—it was the time of coupons when we never threw anything away—and found a little round velvet cap and a suit to match which she had when she was younger. When Catherine put them on, she looked like an adolescent princess on her way to a select boarding-school.

"I'll see what I can do to smarten them up," said Biddy, who had completely thawed in the wedding atmosphere.

Next morning, when Catherine left, she had three cotton roses and an immense veil pinned on to the little cap; beads and a ribbon bow on the jacket and a piece of fur edging tacked round the collar. She cried a little, because she could not have satin and orange-blossom. We felt melancholy because the bride and bridegroom looked like figures out of a fairy-tale and their wedding was unrelieved Utility.

One week-end, soon afterwards, Lefty and Bob asked service contemporaries, who were still not demobilized, to stay. I thought that if the Colonel happened to be haunting the New Wing that night he would be gratified to see the uniforms draped over the chairs.

I had an uneasy idea that I could hear footsteps on the drive when I put the baby to bed after his last feed. I concluded that Howard must be having a midnight prowl.

But next morning, when I went into the kitchen, Reg was sitting there.

"I didn't know you were getting leave," I said.

"I haven't. I skipped."

"Do you mean you've deserted?"

"I shall go back tomorrow," he said.

Catherine told me, as we cleared the breakfast, that Reg had been getting anonymous letters telling him to watch out for his wife. "He took off his boots and tiptoed over the grass with a knife in his hand to look in my bedroom window," said Catherine admiringly.

"Catherine, you must make him go back at once if he doesn't want to be court-martialled."

She came back from the kitchen to say he had promised he would go tomorrow.

The Wing-Commander and the Naval Captain were helping to pick late apples in the garden. They were very sympathetic.

"Suppose you tell him we both order him to go back to his unit at once?" they suggested.

Reg sent a civil reply saying he would certainly return the next day, sir.

We held an agonized conference under the apple-trees.

"Look here," they said. "This is frightfully awkward for us. If we see this absentee here, although we're your guests, we're obliged to have him arrested."

I told Catherine to make sure he never left the kitchen all day. Reg was most obliging and promised to be very careful.

Next morning he went back. Nothing happened. I wondered about the anonymous letters and began to count the weeks until Catherine should go out of Biddy's life.

S.S.A.F.A. were most helpful about Catherine's confinement and arranged for her to go to a very nice country nursing-home. Catherine was haughty and flatly refused.

"But why, Catherine?" I said when the woman had gone.

"I know that place," said Catherine coldly. "I know a girl who went there to have an illegitimate baby. I wouldn't want to be in a place with people like that, Madam."

Eventually we found a place full of guaranteed wives for her, and she packed up and went home to the tied cottage to wait there. There were no more week-end parties for us, it is true, but neither was there the sense of subterranean drama continually surging below-stairs. I asked Howard if there had been as much trouble with Love in the old days, but he said that it was better organized then, and mostly between the maids and footmen. Also, it was then clearly understood that it was a spare-time activity and that work was not suspended on any account. We decided that as the romantic passion was clearly beyond our control, we would stick to Biddy alone for a while, and hope that when her husband got through his gratuity he might think about getting a daily job. Then Biddy announced that she was going to have a baby and was going to live with her husband's mother forthwith. She added that her husband did not like the way she was treated at the manor and never had.

My life was dominated by the boiler. It was the biggest one I have ever seen in a private house. The Colonel and his wife had not been obsessed in any way about washing themselves. There were only two baths in the house and not a single hand-basin of any kind. But they had made up for it in arrangements for having utensils washed. The boiler had to serve the kitchen, the butler's pantry, the scullery, the flower-room, the nursery sink, both bathrooms and two housemaid's pantries. It was like firing the Flying Scotsman. I had to fit in the baby and bedmaking and cooking and cleaning the thirty-three rooms and looking after the other children between stoking sessions.

A little Cornish woman named Gwennie called in answer to my advertisement. Her husband was at the army camp near by and she wanted somewhere to live in the neighbourhood. He moved in with her. He was an odd little Celt, not a bit bigger than her, named Matthew. They were like two nice little trolls, trotting about the five kitchens and talking softly to each other in their burring voices. Gwennie cooked Cornish pasties morning, noon and night, and the others began to grumble. I asked her if she could cook anything else, but she said that the pasties made them feel less homesick, and went on chopping up the vegetables Howard brought in and sealing them up with the week's meat ration and presently we got used to it.

They both applied themselves earnestly to the boiler.

"We'll bust that old soul before we leave," said Matthew.

They did, too. One morning we came down to find the kitchen flooded and a great crack across the cylinder. You couldn't get boilers of that size now, as the men who were called in informed us happily.

"Don't you say nothing to those fellows and I'll fix it," Howard murmured in my ear, as the men got into the lorry and drove away. He and the boy worked all day, with material he unearthed from a locked outhouse and carried up to the house under his apron. By the week-end the taps were running hot water again.

Gwennie got in the family way and went back to Cornwall. I never forget which was the Bulge Year of the British birth-rate, now over-crowding the schools. There is nothing like seeing history actually made, with your own eyes, to impress the dates upon you.

I learned what it was to be physically afraid of the day's hard labour so that my muscles shrank from it. Country housewives seldom suffer from the monotony of their work, simply because it carries real hardships—the biting cold as you go in and out and the heavy lifting and carrying which make you so stupid that rest and warmth are a blissful reward. Without the giant boiler, I could not wash the diapers or the dishes or the children's hands. It was frosty weather and there was an immense network of pipes through and around the house, any one of which could bring disaster upon the surrounding area if it burst.

I got a haunting idea that the house was paying me back for the generations of women who had slaved to keep it clean and warm. There was a dreadful little scullery, with a low stone sink which seemed to break your back in two when you used it. It had a dark window and a stone floor and plaster crumbling off the walls. In the old days there had been one little girl who spent her whole working life in it, standing washing dishes from six in the morning until eleven at night. If I went in there in the half-dark I used to think I saw her, bent over the sink. Seen from below-stairs, the manor looked quite different. I began to think our experiment did not deserve to succeed. The gracious life in the front wing, after all, depended entirely upon service in the back wing, and it didn't seem a justifiable way of living.

The house got thick with dust and the baths sticky with tidemarks and the children wore last week's dirty clothes. But somehow the nine of us had to have food and a modicum of warmth. I was always afraid of dropping off to sleep in the daytime and letting the children have an accident. I did not dare to sit down in an armchair because my eyes closed immediately. Several times I woke up to find the children had finished their meal and vanished and that I was alone with my cooling food in front of me.

It was at this time that Timmy found a friend who would let him sleep in his London flat sometimes.

"After all, it saves you work if I decide not to come home," he said. He much disliked the squalor of our present existence, but above all he disliked having to help with the housework. Pottering around a studio and cooking omelets bears very little resemblance to running a manor built on the assumption that there will always be plenty of cheap labour.

He made no definite arrangement. Sometimes he came back at night and sometimes he did not. We used to leave the door unbolted in case he came back on the last train. Often we woke in the morning to find it still unbolted.

It required an uncommonly noisy burglar to wake me, but I did wake. There were footsteps wandering around downstairs and they were not the footsteps of Timmy. The dog Doubtful was doing nothing whatever about it. I reflected indignantly that it was altogether too much to expect me to stand-in for a whole staff and then find that the dog apparently expected me to do his barking for him as well. When I opened my eyes again it was time to feed the baby and stoke the boiler.

The footsteps came again next night and the night after. But by the time we had made up our minds to the impossible effort of pulling our tired muscles into action and facing the icy cold of the hall we had fallen asleep again. Nothing mattered except our weariness.

We bought cigarettes in boxes, then, because it was such a long way to the village to get any if you ran out. It was one of our household amenities. We all subscribed so much extra to the housekeeping and kept a stock in the cupboard. The boxes seemed to go remarkably fast that week.

We never could work out, when the telephone-bill came in, who owed for which calls. We had put a tin money-box by the telephone and were all on our honour to pay cash for each rail as we made it. The burglar found the box. He used to make a terrible noise shaking the coppers out, because it was one of those boxes that you fill and then break open and throw away. Once, muttering irritably and sleepily I got up and went downstairs to stop him. But he ran out of the door as I came across the landing. I heard his hob-nailed boots clattering down the frosty drive. I remembered Matthew clattering to and from the coal-cellar, stoking up the boiler.

We bolted the front door in order to get some sleep, but it meant that Timmy did not. He picked that night to come home and threw stones at our window for hours and hours. To hear him talk, you would have thought he was the first person ever locked out of an old manor in the snow.

We could not give Timmy a key, because the Colonel's anti-burglar arrangements had been on a scale which did not include gimcrack modern devices of that kind. The front door had no lock, but three huge bolts and a thick chain, and heavy shutters that constituted another door, fastened by a great iron bar in great iron sockets sunk into the stone of the walls. When we first arrived there were burglar-alarms connected to every door and shutter in the house. The children had discovered them, and we were all rather pathological about sudden alarm-signals so soon after the Blitz, so we tore them down. We reflected gratefully how impossible the nights would have been if we still had burglar-alarms, now that we had a real burglar.

We took to keeping only a few pennies, which we did not mind losing, in the telephone-box for Matthew and leaving some Woodbines about for him. Everything would have been all right if only the burglar had been more competent in his chosen profession. Most of our floors were bare, and he clattered most terribly. It was impossible to sleep through his visits. Over and over again I would groan and stir when it seemed only a moment since I had thankfully closed my eyes.

"It's all right. The baby's still asleep. It's only the burglar," my husband would mutter drowsily. Sometimes I toyed with the idea of calling at the camp and asking Matthew if he could not tiptoe or wear rubber shoes. But I could never settle how to open the conversation.

One night he overreached himself. I heard him muttering angrily because he could not get the pennies out. Then I heard a lot of scraping and squeaking and then he clattered off. I thought that as I was awake I might as well bolt the front door now. It was too late for Timmy to come. As I staggered drowsily through the hall, I noticed that Matthew had broken the telephone-box open and left the wrecked tin on the floor. I reflected that someone ought to have taught him the story of the goose that laid the golden eggs along with rules about private property.

In the morning Howard said to me:

"I don't want to say nothing, Madam, but the back door was left open last night."

"I bolted it myself from the inside," I said.

"It was wide open when I came in to get the hens' mash," he insisted.

When I went round opening up the house for the day, I found that Matthew had evidently slept on the drawing-room sofa. Also he had been sick on Diana's only good coat, which she had left there when she went to bed. Since our return to squalid living, we had given up our reformed tidy habits.

In the first flush of annoyance, Diana insisted on the police being told.

The policeman listened in silence and went straight up to the camp. When the M.P.'s approached the topic, Matthew at once opened his kit and handed over the empty cigarette-boxes. The days before the court case we all went round looking at Diana as if she was a pariah.

"If you had only got up and told him to stop burgling, it would never have happened," she said angrily. "Anyway, leaving doors unbolted is just making it difficult for burglars to go straight."

"If Timmy would only keep regular habits, we could bolt doors."

"If only I could rely on finding a meal ready and my bed made, I could keep regular habits," said Timmy.

But it was no use arguing. Somehow poor little Matthew had got entangled in the web of our experiment in living and had got to pay for it. One of the reasons why it is impossible to go back to the old system of domestic service in any form, today, is because there is no way of returning to the obligations which employer had towards employed. They are all looked after by welfare organizations which is obviously a better plan. But once you have domestic staff in the house, without feeling that it is your tiresome duty to see that they behave themselves and remember the ten commandments, someone pays. It was terrible to think that it was Matthew, who used to make me cups of stewed tea when I was working late at night, and stare at me, as he sipped his, with his black eyes twinkling with amusement that any woman should sit up typing instead of going to bed at the proper time like Gwennie.

Matthew grinned at us cheerfully across the court, and all was going well until it came to the question of how he had got out of the house. The fact that he had unbolted a door, instead of just wandering in and out of doors left open already apparently put the whole thing on a different footing and turned it into breaking and entering instead of just entering. Everyone began to look serious and Matthew turned puzzled, despairing eyes on us. We wished someone would explain to the magistrate that if you take little Celtish trolls out of their western villages and away from their wives and recruit them in an army where scrounging is an entirely allowable activity, it is not fair to haul them into a court and turn shocked and moral about it. My husband, who had been fidgeting for some time, got up and said to the magistrate:

"Might I be allowed to say a word, sir?"

There was a stir in the court and the magistrate looked astonished. After some whispered consultations, my husband was waved up to the witness-box and allowed to hold forth.

"I only wanted to say that he lived with us for a long time and was used to coming home at night, so it wasn't really like breaking into a *strange* house," said my husband carefully. "I mean, it does make a difference, doesn't it, sir?"

The magistrate reflected and said that it did.

Matthew was a free man once more. We all crowded round congratulating him outside the court-house. The Welfare Officer stood by smiling benignly.

The policeman said to me next day:

"Matthew's in jail again."

"But I've just written to Gwennie to say he's out."

"He was celebrating having got off last night," said the policeman. "The M.P.'s carried him back to the camp soon after the pub closed."

The Welfare Officer and the policeman between them arranged for me to see Matthew.

"I was just lying on the pavement in front of the pub when someone came by and trod on my face," Matthew explained.

"It might happen to anybody," I agreed sadly.

Matthew got a stiff sentence. He wrote to us from the prison saying it was a bit short on cigarettes and reading matter. We clubbed together and sent him some Woodbines and magazines hoping against hope that he would be allowed to have them. Also we took to bolting the door and letting Timmy take a chance on getting in if he came home. Timmy was irritated and said that if we were going to turn the manor into an institution designed to help the local criminals to avoid temptation it was a pity we hadn't said so in the first place. But he felt as bad about Matthew as any of us and readily agreed to a compromise to bolt it only after Matthew finished his sentence and returned to the camp.

The day he got out, he came round to tea. He had it with the children in the playroom. After he had left, they moped around with very long faces.

"Mummie, they shouldn't be cruel to people in prisons," said Jane.

"They're not allowed to be."

"Matthew told us they have lumpy porridge every single day and sometimes it's burnt as well," said Jane, wide-eyed with horror.

"Let it be a lesson to you to keep straight," I said severely.

One evening shortly before Christmas, a strange girl turned up at the house, with a case in one hand and a turkey in the other. She said she was Biddy's sister from Ireland and had come over to marry her boy, who had just been demobilized. She said this boy was the great love of her life and she had waited for him ever since he was called up. She had come to stay with Biddy until the wedding.

I explained that Biddy didn't live here any more and that she should go to Hertford, to the mother-in-law's residence. Biddy's sister, whose name was Mollie, said that she couldn't do that because she had given Danny this address. She couldn't write to him because he drove a lorry all over the country and had settled to drive it here. The turkey was from her mother in Ireland who raised them on the farm.

Mollie cooked the turkey for us on Christmas Day. It was a wonderful one, fat and white and not in the least like the miserable birds which hung outside the shops this side of the Irish Channel. Mollie did not go in for reading books, nor did she care for the radio. She whiled away the time by scrubbing the house and polishing the wood and stoking the boiler and doing the baby's washing. She said diffidently that she did prefer to be able to see through windows and took a ladder and a lot of rags and let the sunshine into the manor again.

One night a shower of pebbles rattled on our bedroom window. We were not all obsessed about getting some sleep at any price, since Mollie's arrival, and got up promptly, thinking it must be Timmy. But it wasn't. It was a strange lorry-driver.

"Danny's my name," he said, blinking at the sudden light as we let him in. We put him in the butler's bedroom, suggesting that he could get his marriage settlements drawn up at leisure the next day.

He and Mollie were closeted for a long time next morning. At midday I found Mollie alone. She said that Danny had gone away and she didn't know when he would be back. An inquiry about the wedding date froze on my lips, because she looked so impenetrable. She was a very handsome girl, with thick black hair and a white skin. Privately, I thought that Danny hadn't the sense to know when he was on to a good thing.

Mollie spoke no word of returning to Ireland, but continued to polish the wood and do the washing and keep the boiler going and sweep the rooms and scrub the floors. Once I approached the question of the future, but she answered that she had waited for Danny all these years and looked so tragic that I left it until time should have marched on a little. At the end of the week I gave her what I used to give Biddy and she put it away and went on polishing the four Evangelists.

The policeman called and asked to speak to me.

"I know a girl who would do for you," he said. "Shall I send her along?"

Noel was quiet and smiling, rosy and brown-eyed. She said she had been in service at the doctor's for three years, but thought she would like a change. When I asked her why, she said they were all very nice indeed and she was very happy there, but just wanted a change.

At that time, the Welfare State was beginning to take shape and we still had an exhilarating feeling that we were launched on a new world. It didn't match up at all with the log fires in the front wing of the manor and wage-slaves at the back, and the terrible little scullery haunted by the girl who had once washed up there from dawn until midnight. On the other hand, we had learned that you could not live in the house without service. It had been built for one group of people to be served by another, and nothing would alter that. Every square foot of the great building silently insisted that this was the only way to live. The kitchens were deliberately built as far as possible from the family rooms. If I went to the kitchen, I had to take the baby with me, because leaving him behind in the south wing was like leaving him at one end of a row of houses while I went to the other.

Barbara Castle, who was part of the new Labour Government, came down for the week-end and gave us some constructive advice, and between us we worked out a scheme which would enable us to go on living in the manor—now looking breathtakingly lovely with the approach of Spring—and yet not feel that we were saboteurs in the path of progress.

We pored over labour regulations and introduced them whether the manor liked it or not.

First, Mollie and Noel must have a forty-hour week, like everyone else in the brave new world. We spent days and days working out time-sheets, and if you have ever tried to whittle down housework to minutes, you will know that you begin to feel you are engaged in some absurd and impossible task which doesn't make sense, like an uneasy dream. Bob was deeply interested in it, because during the war he had been engaged on the same sort of thing for the whole Air Force, but he said that had been much easier.

"If you knocked five minutes off Mollie making the bed in the East Room on Thursdays and allowed only fifteen for Noel to peel the potatoes on Saturday morning, they could both lie in for an extra ten minutes on Sunday," he would say, sitting, with his mug of cider, in front of the time-sheets pinned to the Butler's Pantry wall.

It was established that Mollie and Noel were paid to run the kitchens of the manor and keep the thirty-three rooms in order, but not to be at anyone's beck and call. Just at this moment, Violet Markham produced her White Paper on Domestic Service, which was the foundation of the House-worker Training Scheme. By great good luck I was asked to take part in a radio discussion with her, to celebrate its launching and she explained her idea of an up-to-date pattern of domestic help. She said that the whole plan would collapse unless we bound ourselves to take the maids' hours of work as seriously as if they had been workmen called in from outside. The temptation to take your own home-made timetable lightly is very acute. Also, there is a wide difference between employing someone to do a certain range of household jobs and calling on them informally to do something for you which you are too lazy to do for yourself. We settled firmly that we could pay Mollie and Noel, out of our joint earnings, to run the house for us, but that to ask them to wait on us would be bourgeois. Timmy and Diana took this very hard.

"What, no morning tea?" they asked plaintively.

My own morning tea was the only thing which could bring me to the baby's first feed in the kind of humour in which a child would wish to find his mother, so I weakened. We solved the problem by deciding that on the mornings on which Noel brought the tea, she should also deliver a cup to Mollie, lying luxuriously in bed, and that Mollie, in her turn, should do the same for Noel.

The most surprising fact, in the whole of this true story about the manor is that the time-sheets worked. Mollie and Noel might be simple country girls, but their fathers and brothers and sweethearts were ruled by shifts and time-charts and overtime money and they fell into the pattern without a word of explanation. There were some mornings on which the commuters had to catch a train which left Ashford at 7.10. This meant either Noel or Mollie getting up at six. Whenever they did this, they got time-and-a-half. Sometimes, if one of them wanted extra money for something, she would start a drive to make the commuters catch the early train so that she could earn it.

Some of our week-end guests were very funny about the time-sheets and the shift system and the legitimate tea breaks. The fact remained that we came nearer to building a new pattern of living on our old foundation then than at any other time we were in the manor. During the whole blissful two years of the Mollie-Noel era, we never had a meal late, never had a meal spoiled, were never called late in the morning and never had to grumble about the way the house was kept. There was never an uncivil word exchanged between family and staff and never a quarrel in the kitchen. When I went round the house, locking up for the night, I always found a scrawled note on the kitchen table from the one who had done the last shift and gone to bed, to the one who had been to the pictures and was therefore due to do the first shift of next day. "She says poach the eggs for breakfast, and Mr. Timmy is home and wants calling"—or whatever it was. The note always ended, "God bless you. Good night."

They presented a united front against Howard and the boy, and were always grumbling that the potatoes were too large or alternatively too small, and that the kindling wasn't dry enough to start the fires. Their pet spare-time hobby was to try and catch Howard out, and they made a point of eating only the early plums which he regarded as sacred to the family. They cruelly mocked the stammering gardener's boy and seemed surprised when I said it was unkind. Howard gladly fell back into the habit of a lifetime and was always resignedly astonished at the inadequacies of those girls in the kitchen. There was a continual chorus of complaints against the rival below-stairs party, and we took it in turns to referee rather absent-mindedly. A great peace descended on the manor, because we had restored the essential Balance of Power. Howard and the boy, Mollie and Noel took up the old feud, which had raged, from time immemorial, between kitchen and garden, with the family in their proper place as mere pawns in the game. Howard illustrated his complaints with nostalgic references to other girls of the past, who had committed the identical crimes in which Mollie and Noel were engaged. They decorated the old Servants' Hall with picture postcards and snapshots of their boys, and took it in turns to use it for petting sessions. We were all firmly convinced that the high illegitimacy rate among domestic servants was at least partly due to the furtiveness imposed upon their courtships and took pains to respect their privacy. Howard prophesied disaster, but for once he was wrong. They were both firmly and calmly married long before there was any idea of an heir. There were times when I felt that the ghost of the little scullery-maid was laid at last.

6

"PITY you don't use that pig-sty," said the policeman.

"We keep bicycles in it."

"You ought to keep pigs in it." We realized that he had called at the manor merely in order to say so.

"Are we allowed to?" we asked, because most simple country pastimes were forbidden by law. But the policeman, conscientiously learning up new regulations in the long winter evenings had discovered that if you formed a village Pig Club you not only got permits for their food but permission to have them killed when they were the right size. "And then the Government takes the carcase?" we suggested cautiously.

He said that the government only took half, in order to feed those not enterprising enough to have their own pig club, and gave you back the rest. Also, with what they paid you for the requisitioned half you could buy two little pigs and start again.

"I'll bet there's a snag in it," said Lefty, deeply interested.

But the more we thought about it, the more we liked it. We had been long enough in the country now to know that keeping a pig somehow stands for stability, just as the most respected citizens of an outer suburb are buying their house on mortgage. If you keep a pig, you are established as thrifty and reliable. The traditional Arithmetic is that you always keep two, one to eat and one to pay overheads and start you again, and the government was evidently taking this as basis for their scheme.

Lefty said there was a lot of money in pigs, properly handled. Bob began to take measurements of the sty, with the idea of working out a complete new drainage system. My husband, who likes trying other people's jobs better than anything else in the world said that he had often fancied a swineherd's life must be a particularly happy one. Timmy said it was a well-known Sunday afternoon pastime to take visitors to scratch the pigs' backs. But the policeman said that as long as he wore the King's uniform no one was going to get away with that as their legal chore. If you belonged to a pig club and failed to take your share of the dirty jobs, you were for it from the government.

We asked Howard if he would like to join the pig club. He looked reproachful.

"You mean me join a club with some of those people from the village in it?" he asked incredulously.

We were afraid he would make trouble about the village members coming in and out to stare at or to feed their share of pig, but most fortunately the pig-sty was on the right-of-way. This was a path from the back drive into the field which ended up at the foot of the railway embankment. No one ever used it, because it did not lead to anywhere, and also because everyone had forgotten about it except Howard. He was always reminding us ominously that if people should take to wandering through the garden in hordes, day and night, we should not be able to stop them.

We drew lots as to whose bacon ration should be surrendered in order to draw meal ration for the pigs and it fell to Diana. She said coldly that it nauseated her so much to think of giving her food up to an animal for the purpose of eating it herself later on that she did not suppose she would ever touch bacon again in any case. We put the bone-meal in the barn, and the policeman bought and installed two little pigs. They looked just like the pictures in Beatrix Potter books. I got the baby out of bed so that he could see them. Their tails curled; they were pink and clean and they frolicked about the sty, squealing and squeaking as if they were being paid for it.

For weeks, there was so much competition to feed the pigs that the village members hardly needed to come down. Then, slowly, the facts of life began to dawn on us. Pigs grow bigger very fast indeed and the bigger they are the more they eat. At first Bob made them troughs just right for their size, and a larger one later and so on. But at last he got tired of it and found an old water cistern in the outhouse and dragged it into the sty and left it there.

They finished their government ration at a mouthful now, with an impatient air, as though they disliked wasting time on hors-d'oeuvres. We boiled up the household scraps and gave them to the pigs instead of the hens, and bought potatoes by the sack and boiled them, but still they were groaning and screaming with hunger. It began to be dangerous to feed them. As soon as they heard the click of a bucket they started battering on the sty gate and the first man who went in was knocked down and trampled underfoot. Bob invented a decoy bucket on a hoist which you let down over the half-door, and then, as they rushed for it, you dashed in and poured their real meal into the trough and dashed out again. We cut all the nettles we could find and threw them into the sty. But they still clearly intended to eat the first one of us they found alone.

Lefty found a firm in London who made a mixture called Tottenham Pudding and sold it by the ton. The men dumped it in the yard, like a hill of steaming copper-coloured mud, smelling sickly. It looked as if it would last the pigs their lifetime. But in no time at all it was finished, and then there was an agonizing gap while we waited for the next delivery. By now the other pig clubs which were springing up all over the place had discovered it. Also, it was terribly expensive and the pig club books showed an alarming deficit. We had to earn extra in order to support them, if the scheme was not to go bankrupt in its first decade. We cut the cucumbers in the greenhouse and never even tasted them ourselves, but gave them to Lefty to take up to London and sell to a West End greengrocer. Then we had a stroke of luck. It rained for several days and then turned very warm, and all the fields sprouted with mushrooms. We spent the whole week-end going round the fields and gathering them. We had Sir Gordon Wilmer, the youngest judge, and his wife, that week-end. He had come down for a rest. But when he heard the pigs wailing for Tottenham Pudding, he at once agreed to spend the week-end on their troubles, and never stopped gathering mushrooms from Friday till Sunday. It was particularly nice of him because what he really wanted to do was to watch the trains go by, which made him happier than anything else in the world, but he said he would take over the fields near the embankment and observe them as he gathered. By the end of the two days, we had got several sacks full of mushrooms, which Lefty said he could sell to a restaurant in London. We sorted them out into good and indifferent, and made the indifferent ones into Mushroom Ketchup, which tasted like brine and which we never could bring ourselves to use but left in the larder for several years and then threw away. Lefty brought £3 home from the restaurant proprietor with a curt message that his customers would not look at another omelette or devil-on-horseback for at least a year from now. I sent some lettuces and currants to Ashford market, but the disadvantage of living in Kent is that you cannot even give fruit and vegetables away locally most of the year, and although people are longing for them in London the cost of transport puts any amateur grower in the red if he tries to sell them there. The garden was thick with roses, and our lettuces were bolting and had to be given to the hens, but there was no way of getting them to London to sell except for the commuters to take them up in baskets, which made them all late at their offices.

We had thought, when we started to keep pigs, that we should be able to have interesting discussions about their progress, as the farmers and the genuine squires (as opposed to the Green Line squires) did. But we found that we talked about nothing except where to get them some food, and we talked of that endlessly. Sometimes, when the others were in London and they were snorting and battering at the sty door I used to get into a panic. It is dreadful to have animals on your hands which you cannot feed. The village members brought bits out of their gardens, but we never had enough.

Just as we were in despair, the director of a film company rang up. He said he was making a film about "William" and there was a sequence in it about William letting some pigs into a garden. Would our pigs care to star in it? They would be well paid. I instantly bargained for a higher fee and closed the deal. The film people came down next day and the pigs spent all morning rehearsing and the afternoon shooting, and came in tired and very hungry. I spent their salaries on two sacks of "chats"—that is potatoes too small for human consumption.

Gilbert Harding came down that week-end. He arrived in an aggrieved frame of mind on account of the antics of a mother and baby on the train. After he had gone up to bed he came down again in his dressing-gown and said, "Since I am so clearly unwelcome here I propose to take the first train back to London tomorrow morning." But next morning he went down with the others to feed the pigs and after that he hardly set foot indoors again until Monday morning. He simply could not bear to watch them snuffling around the trough, hoping to find a forgotten crumb after their meal. He found some bricks at the bottom of the garden and built an outdoor stove and gathered wood and lit a fire in it, and got an old bucket and boiled potatoes in it all week-end and gave them to the pigs. Sunday afternoon was bleak and grey and I went down to the stableyard to suggest he came indoors and had tea. He was sitting watching the bucket boil with a far-away expression like a holy man sitting on top of a pillar in the desert. He said gently that he hoped no one would feel wounded if he didn't join the party but he was just discovering what contentment lay in supplying food to simple, grateful creatures. He was so benign that he occasionally tossed a potato over the wires to the hens, though he was not fond of them. This was the happiest week-end of the pigs' lives.

When the policeman inspected the pigs that week, he said we should begin to work on getting a permit. At that time there was a great deal of illegal slaughtering going on. If the farmers wanted to give a party, they used to tell the inspector that one of their lambs had broken a leg and therefore had to be slaughtered and they were just making sure the meat was not wasted, as they could not have got a permit through to sell it before it went bad. Our policeman spent most of his day, at the moment, cycling round the countryside making sure that all pigs were still alive and in their sties. Even with his knowledge of the ropes, it seemed a long time trying to supply enough food for ours before the permit came through.

The men from the Ministry arrived one morning when I was on my own with the baby. They drove nonchalantly up to the pig-sty door, unfastened the back of the lorry, put a gangway down to the pig-sty door, opened the door and invited the pigs to walk up it. I was so amazed at the reckless and foolhardy procedure that I stood, clutching the baby, frozen to the spot. The pigs instantly dashed off into the undergrowth. I ran as fast as I could up to the house, with the baby screaming with laughter. I took him into the drawing room and put the bars up over the shutters. I listened for a long time, hoping to hear the lorry drive away and fearing to hear the screams of the men from the Ministry as the pigs trampled them down and took a few mouthfuls. At last I talked myself into going out again. I locked the drawing-room door and put the key in my pocket. Then I took it out and put it prominently on the hall table in case I never came back.

The two men were pouring with sweat and sitting on the footboard of their lorry. I asked where the pigs were. They said despondently that they thought one had gone into the orchard but they had no information about the other.

By great good luck, two city slickers drove up at that moment, with the object of trying to interest me in a vacuum cleaner. I suppose they were not accustomed to receiving the kind of welcome from housewives which they got from me. They followed me dazedly down to the lorry and took off their natty jackets and hung them carefully on the pig-sty wall.

We made an ambush round the orchard and wriggled through the undergrowth and trapped the pig in a narrowing circle, like Red Indians. Then it looked up, carefully spotted the weakest link in the circle and made a dash in my direction. Two things struck me in the split second of its charge, with its wicked little eyes glaring at me. The first was a remark of Howard's, made long ago, "Pigs don't bite; they chop". The other was that we had made no arrangements whatever about how to deal with the pig once we got to the point of catching it. It thundered past me and disappeared again. The atmosphere was heavy with reproach, but no one spoke until one of the men from the Ministry said, with some restraint, that it was a well-known fact that exercise was not good for pigs about to be slaughtered. In the distance, we saw the pig pausing to scratch itself against the heavy oak fence, which collapsed like a child's castle of bricks.

The city slickers got together and thought up a scheme for putting a wire-netting trap among the bushes and driving them into it. We all got ourselves rakes and yard-brooms out of the tool-shed. By lunch-time we had got one manoeuvred back into the pig-sty and were at least half-way back towards the point at which we had first started. The other city slicker had a brilliant idea, and at his suggestion I fetched a bucket of food from indoors and strewed scraps invitingly up the gangway and stood the bucket at the top. On that, the pig walked up the gangway and into the lorry. Some sixth sense told the other there was food about, and it emerged from the rose-garden and dashed up the gangway too. The men did up the tail-board and hurriedly drove away. One of the vacuum-cleaner men was bleeding all over the path so I took him indoors to bandage him up. I was so grateful that I invited them to tell me all about the vacuum cleaner and how it worked, and show me all the brushes in turn. But they only stared limply at me, and dried off the sweat on the bath-towel and went out to their car in silence. They never came back again. What is more I never had a single man trying to sell me a cleaner again, all the time I was at the manor, and before that I used to get a great many. I couldn't help wondering if salesmen marked the gate, like tramps, and if ours had the strongest code warning of all.

I had not been prepared for our half of the meat to come back looking so like a pig. The Ministry apparently did not want their heads, and so there were two, looking at me as if bitterly remembering how I had tricked them into the lorry, every time I went into the larder. I told Mollie and Noel to keep the larder door locked because I didn't want the children to have nightmares about Bluebeard's chamber. I tried lying the heads down on the shelves, instead of sitting up on their necks, but they looked just as bad. I tried covering them with muslin, but it looked so sinister that you had to lift the cloth and then you wanted to scream. I thought I had found a way out when I fetched two glowing Orange Pippins from the store and fixed one in each snout. But it didn't look so much gay and medieval as obscene.

I put the children all to bed early and said I was going to do some cooking and they must go straight off to sleep and not bother me. They asked what I was going to cook and I talked vaguely of sausage rolls.

Mollie was out, and when I took the heads into the kitchen Noel said she had a headache and would write letters in bed if it was all the same to me. I lit a cigarette and thought how strange it was that butchers chose their vocation.

To my dismay, the door opened slowly and Colin appeared in his pyjamas. I looked at him speechlessly. I could hardly have felt worse if I had just done the throat-cutting myself. Colin came slowly round and looked at one head. Then he went over and pushed his face almost into the snout of the other. A smile of pure joy spread over his face.

"*That's* the one that once knocked me down," he said. "Hooray, hooray. Are the sausage rolls ready yet?"

All next day and the day after, the smell of lard spread through the house and up the stairs and into the bedrooms. We woke feeling sick, looked with revulsion at our breakfast bacon and developed a passion for lemon juice. I made pork pies, with hot lard poured into the flour, and solid pork inside and was gratified to find that the jelly formed and made the pies look exactly like the one we used to have on Christmas Day at home, long ago before the first world war. I cooked basinfuls of brawn, and we ate liver for two solid days. The factory had sent back sausages and when we had them for breakfast it was a revelation of how much sawdust we had been eating for years.

The sides of bacon had been cured at the factory, and we hung them on a hook which the Colonel had provided for this very purpose. They got maggots in them, so that you had to dodge past when you went into the larder, if you didn't want them on yourself. We got so that we didn't mind them at all after a while. Every Saturday afternoon we took the sides of bacon out on to the lawn and brushed the maggots off and nibbed more salt into the bacon. Once two immensely glamorous females, in a car with a liveried chauffeur drove in, supposing it to be the home of the famous dress designer. We absent-mindedly went up to the windows of the car with our sides of bacon, brushing away, to direct them to his quaint little cottage over the hill. But half-way through our directions they leaned back in their seats, shuddering, with handkerchiefs to their mouths and called to the chauffeur to drive off at once.

It was wonderful to have a whole side of bacon hanging in the larder. Whenever we were short of a meal we simply went in with a knife and hacked a great piece off and cooked it. One of our regular week-end dishes was a great hunk of it, roast, with hot raisin sauce. When the Ministry finally disgorged what they owed us, we never hesitated but bought two more little pigs and started again. But from then on, we cured the bacon ourselves. Everyone laughed at us, but we bought an out-of-date cookery book and followed its directions scrupulously, collecting all the various herbs and spices from different shops until we had them all, and not skipping any of the complicated directions. Like most old-fashioned cookery books, this one assumed you had the whole twenty-four hours free for the job, and was very firm about the time that had got to be spent on rubbing in salt-petre and spices every day. There was no one person who had the time, but between us we had, and we made a strict rule that whenever one of us set foot in the larder, if it was only to get milk for a cup of tea, he had to massage the bacon. The grocer, who examined it one afternoon when he came to deliver goods, was very contemptuous about our curing and said we should have sent it to the factory, where they had modern short cuts to preserving. The fact remained that the bacon we cured ourselves never got a single maggot in it, whereas once, when we had sent some to the factory again it came back already wriggling about and we summoned the sanitary inspector who was not interested in the very least. Our success with the curing somehow encouraged us all round about our experiment in taking the manor between us. It was proved that there were some things better done by conscientious amateurs like ourselves.

That summer was our heyday. We branched out in all directions. Now that the pigs had been so successful, we decided to embark on geese. They had a moveable wire run on what had once been the tennis court. Every evening, when I put the baby to bed at dusk, I would wait at his window to watch Colin drive the geese in for the night. When he unlatched the wire, they would spread their wings, slowly and begin to move. First they would take a few running steps, then crouch again, like curtseying dancers. Then they would all begin to go faster, with a gliding movement, beating their wings. Then came the climax, when they covered the last bit of the lawn completely airborne. Their great white wings and their long necks, and the dark trees beside the lawn and the sunset sky behind them, and the slow grace of their progress made it so like a ballet that I used to fancy they were moving to music which I could not hear from the window. Colin used to run behind them, his arms outstretched and his hair flying as though, when he reached the edge of the lawn, he would become airborne too.

They never laid a single egg, and I never could see that they kept the grass down on the tennis court, as they were supposed to, but merely trod it down into muddy squares the size of the run. But they taught me that, however comical a goose looks, waddling about the henyard, it is breathtakingly graceful and beautiful flying with outstretched neck against the sunset.

That summer, too, we had time to attend to the river, which flowed through our garden and on to Canterbury, where foreign tourists were never tired of riding on it in hired boats. Bob bought a flat-bottomed invasion boat for us, and we paddled upstream under the railway and among the wide fields and bought driftwood and water-lilies home. The children fell in so often that, even though the river was shallow we thought they had better learn to swim. We found that beyond the railway the water fell over a weir and made a natural bathing-pool below it, and went up there to bathe regularly. When the Golden Arrow flashed by, on its way to

Paris, we would see the faces in the dining-car all twist round at once and stare back at us.

Lefty sent for his old fishing-rod and caught eels and tried to persuade Noel to make them into pies. Once, after a gale, we found our boat held up by a tree that had fallen across, and we cut it away from its roots and hauled it out. Howard promised to say nothing to the Catchment Board about this officious assumption of their duties and we sawed the tree up to use in the winter. Bob cut some large sticks and some small, short ones and taught us all how to play tip-cat. You lie one of the small blocks across the trunk and hit it at one end with a large one, to make it jump into the air and then give it a great bat as it comes down. It is the Saxon origin of cricket and is one of those games which is so fascinating, once you start it, that it is no wonder at all that the Saxons made no real impression on Britain's forests. Once the doctor called to stitch someone up while we were playing and got so wedded to the game that he had to be fetched back to do the bit of stitching. The farmer stopped to watch one day, on his way to the shed for his hay-cutter, and said we ought to get up a team to play against the village cricket club. In no time at all we found ourselves committed to the idea.

My husband volunteered to ask some B.B.C. people down to make up our eleven, and this threw the village cricket club into a frenzy of anticipation. It was like a fairy-tale to them, that they should actually bowl to the owners of the disembodied voices which filled their cottage kitchens every night.

They practised so hard that my husband got nervous and threw out some of the B.B.C. people he had asked because they were particular friends of his and substituted others known to be handy with a cricket bat. The farmer's wife and I got together to supply the lunch and I was not at all surprised to learn that one of the farmer's lambs had carelessly fallen down in the field and broken a leg the very same day that one of his pigs had come an identical cropper in the farmyard. The larder of the manor began to look positively medieval, with saddle of mutton and legs of pork. We undertook to supply a barrel of cider, though the farmer was oddly reluctant about this. We gathered that he despised the ordinary cider, because it had no body in it, like real farmhouse cider. He said the cider he kept at his farm was the very quickest way of taking your legs from under you, if that was what one happened to be wanting. We were alarmed and stuck to our resolution to supply the drinks ourselves. Noel and Mollie's young men from the village volunteered to come and help serve the lunches of their own accord and came down the day before to assist Mollie and Noel to pull tables and chairs about, which was a blessing, because the Elizabethan refectory tables needed four or five people to move them. We had three in all, and on this occasion we put them all in the dining-hall and spread them with the good white linen which had been part of my grandmother's trousseau seventy years before.

My husband insisted on his team coming down the night before, as he said he would not have them take the field tired from a journey when the village team had done nothing but cram the day's farm work into the first three hours of the morning. Even the manor seemed to bulge a little, with eleven extra in the house, and Freddie Allen had to sleep on a sofa instead of a bed and got up looking heavy under the eyes, and saying he felt sick. We rang the policeman, who came down to look Freddie over and said that although he personally was backing the village, in the interests of British justice Freddie ought to have some rum. We had nothing but cider in the house. The policeman reflected and remembered a pub which was vague in the extreme about licensing laws, and two fellow-members of the team drove Freddie there and brought him back looking calm and resolute.

I kept on meeting strange women on the stairs and wondering who they were, as they said nothing at all to me. It turned out that they were B.B.C. wives who had come down on the early train to see the match and brought down various female friends with them. I suppose they all had lunch, as the farmer's supplies were inexhaustible and I know they had tea, because I came down from the match during the afternoon, to get the baby up from his rest, and found them sitting drinking it in the drawing-room, but I never discovered who they all were.

Laurence Gilliam went in first, with Freddie. Laurence said he hadn't touched a bat since he was at the university and hardly remembered which end of it was which. But no one could get him out and by lunch-time he was still slogging away, with the tail of the B.B.C. team at the other end. The farmer was gloomy because he had counted on getting all the B.B.C. out long before midday. After lunch he sought out Laurence and asked if he would care to see over the farm and took him off in his car. Laurence told us afterwards that for all he knew the farm consisted of one small brick-walled room with a jar of cider in it. The farmer kept on plying him with it and looking at his legs so that Laurence began to wonder if there were moth-holes in his college cricket flannels. But eventually they had to come back to the cricket-ground and Laurence strode to the wicket telling my husband privately that he was going to send catches now because he thought the B.B.C. had had the field long enough and anyway his muscles were ready to crack after the first exercise they had had these twenty years.

He hit out wildly but the ball simply wouldn't rise. It kept on shooting straight into the nettles beyond the boundary, and the fielders got rattled and were always standing anywhere except in its path. Laurence's score piled up and up, and the sweat began to pour off him, but still, every time the ball touched his bat off it went, clean and fast and low. At last he took to leaving his wicket unguarded, but this appeared to upset the bowlers so much that they bowled nothing but wides. Finally in response to his agonized signals from the wicket my husband announced that the B.B.C. would declare and let the village fielders have a rest. It has never been settled since, at the B.B.C., whose fault it was that the village won after all.

We were pleased with the festive atmosphere of the cricket match and when the British Legion asked my husband if he could produce some more B.B.C. characters for a village concert he said he would. He didn't want to disappoint the villagers by bringing some small-time variety star or anything like that, so managed to persuade Parry Jones and Ernest Lush to come down and do it as a favour and stay with us for the night. It really looked rather startling on the hand-bills to see their names down to appear in our village hall. The tickets didn't seem to be going so well. The week-end before the concert we discovered to our dismay that hardly enough had been sold to fill the two front rows of chairs. It was embarrassing, because we couldn't ask two people of that eminence to entertain a dozen people, and it was even more difficult to put the concert off. The policeman told us that the village people thought it was not going to be the kind of music they really liked, and talked wistfully about screaming comics they heard in Workers' Playtime. We couldn't force them to come, though by now we were getting so nervous about our coming embarrassment that we would willingly have paid for the seats if they would only sit in them. Then we remembered the parable of the wedding-guests and the highways and hedges, and thought it might work in reverse.

We telephoned all the most prominent people of the district—the M.F.H., the local magistrates, the county families and all the well-known actresses and authors with which Kent is peppered. They all came. The village never had so many elegant cars drawing up as it did that night. It quite consoled them for their own lack of entertainment. Afterwards, a lot of them came back to the manor for cider. We had been warned that the proprietors of the two Kent papers—the *Kentish Express* and the *Kent Messenger*—should not be invited into the same concert hall, unless it was an unusually large one, so were alarmed to find them both standing round the manor fire. However, they fell into animated and affectionate conversation and apparently called the feud off. Sir Charles Igglesden, of the *Kentish Express* was an old, old man who had run the paper for about sixty years and was now reluctantly allowing other people to do a few simple jobs about the office. He talked wistfully of the good old days when the Colonel had driven about the district collecting the manor rents, and before he left arranged with us that we should go to tea with him as soon as his peonies bloomed, because that was a sight we should never forget. But before the peonies showed more than a few bright crinkled edges packed in the green, he was dead.

People who came for the week-end took back tales of our dawn chorus. It was true that any record of bird-songs now sounded, to us, as if half the orchestra was missing and the rest suffering from stage-fright. That summer, too, a nightingale installed itself in the trees by the river. We were not surprised, because we were getting into the frame of mind, about bird-songs, when we thought we were owed a nightingale. Our friends thought we were showing off, but it really was true that we got so much high-class bird-music that we did not consider the nightingale's effort anything out of the ordinary.

David Lloyd-James, who is an expert about bird-songs, used to come down for the week-end and go to bed immediately after supper so that he could be up with his note-book at dawn, identifying the members of the orchestra. He told Ludwig Koch about the manor and Ludwig Koch said he would like to make a record of the chorus. He fixed a day for the recording-vans to come. We hoped it would not be a wet morning.

A few days before the recording date, we vaguely noticed that the farmer was doing some shooting. He had been doing quite a lot lately and we did not pay much attention. But that day some rooks came circling round and round our lawn, for all the world like the Israelite spies of the Old Testament, sent to make a report on the Promised Land. Then the rooks moved in.

They were everything that was disagreeable, including being jerry-builders. They croaked and quarrelled and appeared to be screaming with laughter in their raucous voices as they slung together their untidy black nests. You could not hear any other bird in the garden. We could barely hear ourselves speak in the house.

We sought out the farmer. He was immensely apologetic. He said he had been trying to put the rooks off nesting around his cornfield for years and could not imagine why he had succeeded now. When he knew the whole story, he even came over with his gun and shot down one or two of the new nests, in an effort to convince the rooks that this was not such a healthy site for town-planning either. But it was no use.

Frank and Elizabeth Collinson came by, on their way to Ashford from their own exquisite little manor in the next village, while we were trying to dislodge the invaders and were absolutely horrified. They asked us if we did not know that rooks brought luck to a house like nothing else? Frank and Elizabeth are very strong on folklore and know more of it than any folk ever invented for themselves. They said we must not on any account let the rooks feel unwelcome because if they stayed we should all be in for a straight run of good fortune. We had to ring up Ludwig Koch and he cancelled the appointment. He said a record of rooks cawing would not sell. They paid not the smallest attention to our efforts to remove them, but brought a gang of friends from another colony to join them. Frank and Elizabeth could not have been wronger, about the manor being in for a run of luck.

7

LOOKING back, I date the beginning of our downhill slide to a day when Howard said he wanted to speak to me in the Business Room. In the Colonel's day, this had been the place where tenants came to pay their rent. They used to queue all down the passage as far as the door leading to the little west courtyard, where we now had a trestle table and benches so that we could have supper there with the sunset filling the courtyard like a row of pink footlights directed on to the three white walls of the house around it. Howard had often told us of the day when he was a raw boy, waiting outside the business-room door in a line of even rawer boys, to apply for his first job on the manor.

But now, half a century after, he was getting tired. He told me, in a kind of discouraged surprise, that the nettles seemed to grow faster than they used to and the ground-elder to be tougher and more persistent. He spoke disapprovingly of the Americans letting off the atom bomb and said that he could have told them (if asked) that no good would come of interfering with the weather like that. But he had noticed that nothing had been the same in the manor garden since that ill-advised explosion in the Pacific. There was no sense in green winters and cold summers, such as we were now having. He could assure me for a fact that he was no slower than he ever had been, but with the seasons getting all stream-lined in this way, the garden was out-stripping him. He would have to give it up.

We felt as if the bottom had dropped out of our world. It was not only that Howard could cope with every emergency, from a tap that unaccountably failed to produce water to the dog Doubtful chasing the farmer's sheep. There was something more important than that. It was Howard who had been our essential link with the past. He had taught us to understand the way the machinery of the great house and garden worked. We had imposed our own eccentric plan upon the structure, it is true. But we could not have done that if he had not been there to guide us. We tried to imagine running the manor without Howard. It was impossible.

Howard hastened to reassure us. His cottage had been left to him, by the Colonel, for his lifetime. He would still be on the premises and we could call on him whenever we were in a difficulty. He hoped, he said, to get us really into the way of managing for ourselves before he died. I never welcomed the idea of independence less.

Howard said we must get another man to do the garden, while he drew his pension and kept an eye on things. He had got it all worked out that it wouldn't cost us more than we could afford. The new man would live in the second cottage, now occupied by the bowler hat. This would mean, said Howard anxiously, a dead loss of his fifteen shillings a week rent. Would that, or would it not, ruin our financial arrangements?

I reflected, much touched, that Howard's previous financial concerns had not been on this scale. He had helped the Colonel, when a young man, to retrench after his wild oats had cost forty thousand pounds. Now he never let the garden cost a penny more than we could afford, and spent many pleasant hours thinking up schemes whereby we could save a few shillings. I assured him that we could face the loss of the bowler hat's rent if we were sure of losing the bowler hat himself.

"Don't say nothing for a week," said Howard.

At the end of the week, a small van drew up outside the second cottage, collected some furniture and went away. Some minutes after our tenant emerged and marched down the drive for the last time, and out of our lives for ever. I cannot say there was much of a gap since we had never yet spoken to him.

We swarmed over the empty cottage, examining it curiously. There is nothing more enchanting than finding yourself in possession of a cottage. It offers endless possibilities, from transforming the lives of—say—some Displaced Persons who have long given up hope, down to moving in yourself and saving a lot of money by letting your own establishment. There is something about a little country cottage, set between garden and fields that starts one dreaming wildly of chintz and rocking-chairs and a life without a telephone in it. This was rather a nice cottage, compact and solidly built, with a splendid view of the Golden Arrow from most windows. Although it had the curved gables of the manor, it had evidently been built not long ago. Howard said the Colonel had built it and that he, Howard, used to live in it himself.

"When I was made head gardener, the old head gardener wouldn't move," he explained.

"But didn't the Colonel make him?"

"He wouldn't go," said Howard. "He just stayed there. So the Colonel had to build this one for me."

We pondered this new light on the Colonel and didn't altogether like it. Besides, it aroused a disturbing idea in our minds. If the Colonel had simply crumpled up when faced with the implacable resentment of the old gardener against the new, what hope was there for us? Howard had made it plain that he regarded the gardener's fierce grievance as natural and reasonable. Even if the Archangel Gabriel applied for the job with us, we knew Howard would find fault with his management of the garden.

"There's only one thing for it," we decided. "Howard must pick the new man; then he'll be obliged to make the best of him."

We only got three answers to our advertisement, as you can make a better living for yourself, in Kent, by being a jobbing gardener. Howard chose the third. He was a tall, lean middle-aged man named Morris. Howard told us that when choosing a gardener who was going to live on the premises, one should always take particular note of his wife.

"Of course, you've got to be careful she's agreeable if she's going to be part of the establishment," we agreed. Howard answered that on the contrary the more disagreeable she was the better. If she was a hundred per cent scolder and nagger, her husband would be reluctant to go indoors from the garden. He would, in addition to working the maximum regular hours, drift out frequently at evenings and weekends, whenever she threw a scene. Once there, he would potter about, putting this and that right, just for something to do. Gardeners, said Howard, never, on any account, sit in a garden. It is just a thing that never occurs to them as a possible way of spending the time. Also, most gardeners are good-tempered and placid to the extent of exasperating their wives by never answering back. This almost invariably produces the satisfactory situation of a scold in the gardener's cottage and an eternally pottering exile outside it.

We looked the unspoken question which was in our minds.

He himself, answered Howard, was afflicted with a quiet and sweet-tempered wife, and only his own superhuman devotion to duty had saved the manor up to date. But we could not possibly rely on such a stroke of luck happening twice; therefore he had been careful to make inquiries about Morris's wife.

When Morris moved in, we all regarded her timidly. But she seemed the most silent and imperturbable of women, and so far as we were concerned never earned Howard's opinion of her as the perfect mate for a gardener. Morris, however, was so good-natured and gentle that the ninepence-in-the-shilling boy brightened up and began to improve so much that he was hardly recognizable. He had attached himself passionately to Colin, so that you would hear an endless murmur of conversation from the two of them although none of the rest of us could get him to speak. With Colin to love, and Morris as a patient teacher, his life was transformed. Once a stray dog moved in on us, and after several unsuccessful attempts to make it realize it was unwelcome, Morris proposed that the garden-boy should be allowed to adopt it. After that, you only needed to locate one dog to track down the rest of the party—Morris and the boy, Colin and the other dog. The boy's transformation somehow made a glow of warm satisfaction hang over the manor. We felt as if we had compensated a little for Matthew's misfortune at our hands.

Howard seemed to spend as much time in the garden as he ever did, although he was living on his pension and his means. He called upon us all, continually, to notice how inspired his choice of a new man had been.

As Christmas approached, Howard and Morris cut us a Christmas tree so big that it would hardly stand upright in the drawing-room. Jane's fairy doll, on top of it, had an uneasy look of being jammed against the ceiling. But we needed a big one because presently it emerged that we were giving a staff and tenants' party, just as the Colonel always had done. Howard's married daughter, who was coming to stay, was naturally attending it, as was Morris's old mother-in-law and the current young men of Mollie and Noel. It was just as well someone mentioned it to us. In fact, we only gathered it was all arranged when I happened to ask Noel why she had been keeping everyone's allocation of currants and raisins in a big jar in the larder for several months. She answered matter-of-factly that we should need a big cake for over twenty people on Christmas Day. She added that the Mummers would expect mince-pies at least when they came, so maybe I had better order another few bags of flour and some ingredients for mincemeat and open up some of the tins of fat which my sister had sent us from Kenya.

After the drab and utility Christmases of war-time, we were willing to accept the Dickensian role thrust upon us, even if it ruined us. As a matter of fact we were not so badly off that year. We were discovering that the simple Arithmetic upon which our household was based was working out. If you divide every bill by six, you can face the morning's post, even on quarter-days, with equanimity. But not one of the six of us could have had anything like our standard of living, supporting himself alone. Diana's flat, Timmy's studio, Bob and Lefty's residential club had cost them far more than their share of the thirty-three rooms and four acres. My husband and I needed space for the children to grow up more than anything else, and were able to supply them with a liberty we could never have purchased for them in any other way. It is wonderful to have such a spacious, dignified and picturesque life that all your friends envy you, and know all the time that you are getting it at cut price.

So we were pleasantly resigned to the Squire-at-Christmas role assigned to us and launched on the preparations with enthusiasm. We boiled up a Pig Club ham and decided that the gander was doing nothing much to justify its existence and also that we were tired of being set upon by it if we met it in the garden, and asked Morris to wring its neck. He seemed dismayed and said that geese were not so simple as all that. He. organized all the men of the party, and took them into the barn, with him and the gander, and bolted the doors. They came back looking rather green and sick, and warned me sombrely not to be surprised if the bird started wandering about the larder, as personally they believed it to be immortal. I left it to Mollie and Noel to pluck and they put the feathers away to make pillows for their trousseaux. I put two rings in the Christmas pudding and privately made a note to make sure Mollie and Noel got them, to avoid certain gloom and despondency. As a matter of fact, owing to my sleight of hand, when serving the pudding, not being up to form, Diana got one of them. But it was Lefty who turned red.

Morris and the boy had brought in loads of holly and we picked ivy-leaves off the front gable and made them into daisy-chains and slung them in a star reaching right across the hall and put an enormous log on the fire as a Yule-log.

We shall never like a white Christmas so much as we loved the green Christmases of Kent. There were Christmas roses in the garden, and violets at the foot of the trees beside the river. In the orchard, half a dozen red apples hung, smooth and shining and sound to the core, as we went up to the village church on Christmas morning. In the rose-garden, three or four roses were unwithered on the bare bushes.

As the dusk came down over the mild, moist afternoon, we lit the candles on the Christmas tree and went down to the drive gate to see it blaze in the window of the oldest wing. Morris and his relatives and Howard and his relatives came, marching up the drive and we beckoned them to come in with us. They looked shocked, and Howard told us, in a reproving undertone, that the staff party went in by the back door and joined those girls in the kitchen before coming through to the front of the house. Presently they all emerged into the dining-room from the kitchen entrance, and took their seats at the long table. Colin clutched the hand of the garden-boy and never let it go again all evening.

Afterwards, we all danced around the Christmas tree and distributed presents to everyone. The Mummers came bursting in through the French windows, with their faces blacked, and capered about the room in a way which would have made the Folk Dance Society wince. No one would go home to bed.

We cut cold goose sandwiches when we could not bear our own hunger any longer, and this inspired them all to stay on for another two hours.

We decided to go to Switzerland for ten days. Howard was respectfully approving. It seemed that the Colonel and his wife had a regular routine for going abroad, which was to pack the maids off home with their board wages and leave everything to him. Noel and Mollie, slightly surprised, took their money and went off to visit their families, and Howard was left, once again, to tread the echoing passages at dusk and in the morning, just as he had all the years of the war.

At the last moment Timmy decided not to come. His determination to improve himself and thus make more money to support the manor was working out. Only, he was not using it to support the manor. He was getting well-known now. The village children used to ask him for autographs. Also, all the tradesmen used to refer to the manor as Timmy's place, insinuating that we were only staying with him as long-term guests or poor relations. Timmy liked that. It annoyed the rest of us immensely.

We sent him postcards from Switzerland, telling him about the sunshine and the snow, but we never got any answers.

Once two of us went down from our Swiss mountain village to the town at the foot of the mountains. Some other English tourists sat next to them in the café, and talked to each other, most mysteriously, about a great darkness at home. When we got back to England we found the Fuel Crisis of 1947 in full swing.

The shops in Ashford were lit with candles. In London, people were going straight to bed when they got in from their offices, in order to keep warm.

Now we discovered the advantage of living in a self-supporting community. There was no fuel shortage at the manor. On the contrary, now that the ground was too hard for garden work, Morris and the boy simply spent the day in cutting up logs and bringing them in. The electricity cuts meant nothing to us, because Howard started up the old-fashioned kitchen range and stoked it with wood, and we cooked in its ovens. Mollie had never believed in vacuum cleaners, so that the house was just as clean and neat as usual, while everyone else was trying to do their cleaning in the non-peak hours, when you were permitted to use electricity. Howard dug out hurricane-lamps and old paraffin-lamps and an oil heater from one of his hiding-places. There were enough stored vegetables off the place to keep us all going comfortably, with the sides of bacon in the larder; there were rows of apples in the store above the conservatory and all the fruit we had bottled in the autumn. Once, when the baker's van failed to get through snow-drifts, Mollie baked us Irish farmhouse bread instead.

All our London friends used to ring up, begging to be allowed to come for the week-end, so that they could remind themselves what civilized life used to be like. When they came and found a log fire in their bedrooms and hot roast ham with parsnip sauce and the hot home-made punch simmering in a copper saucepan, they used to think that they must have succumbed to the cold at last and awakened in Paradise.

We discovered, that winter of the fuel crisis, that the pleasures of country life are not limited to the summer. There was an exquisite pleasure in defeating the cold. When you came in from the iron-hard garden and the lane with last night's white frost still on the bare twigs, and saw the fire leaping and heard it crack and crackle, it was a pleasure far sweeter than merely thawing off in a centrally-heated flat. In the evenings, when we bolted the heavy, tight-fitting shutters over the windows, the room would warm up so steadily that presently the shutters themselves were warm to the touch. We left a log on each fire when we went to bed, and in the morning the rooms were still warm, and when you threw another one on to the living ashes they began to stir and set fire to it.

We were so busy, joyfully fighting the emergency, that for a time we did not notice anything was wrong on the manor. Then we began to realize that Howard and Morris were not on speaking terms. The feud embittered our life from then on.

Neither of them would explain it, and if we tried to reconcile them, they behaved as if we had offered the last insult. If we spoke to Howard in the garden, we would see Morris watching us from the potato-plot close by. If we spoke to Morris, we would see the gleam of Howard's white apron from behind the bush, where he would be listening.

For a time, we laughed about it among ourselves and thought they would soon come round. But they never did. It poisoned the atmosphere and it was always with us.

Neither would say what it was about. From the farmer, and from the stammering words of the boy, we at last narrowed it down to being a dispute about whether it was Howard or Morris who had let the stable tap freeze up.

We learned the strength and venom of these country quarrels which never get thrashed out. We began to understand why the Colonel had been driven to build a new cottage. If they had shouted and sworn at each other, or even fought, it would have been less awful than the bitterness they nursed and fostered and kept alive silently. They lived so near to each other that they could hear each other's every movement and tell, from the light on the bedroom ceiling, when the other man had gone to bed. But those two good men never spoke to each other, nor looked each other in the face again until Morris carried Howard's coffin out of the narrow front door so close to his own.

When the frost broke, the river flooded. All the fields were under water and the farmer went around looking like death. Lambs died of pneumonia as soon as they were born. The road was one long watersplash and cars kept on getting stuck and having to be helped out.

But the Colonel's forefathers had been cautious men. They had not even trusted an innocent little river like the Great Stour, which flowed through our garden on its way to Canterbury and then the sea. It might flow meekly and quietly between its high banks for a century or two. But once in a hundred years—who knew—it might take the bit between its teeth and lay waste to the fields. They built the manor deliberately out of its reach, on four acres which stood just above the fields all round them. The muddy water swirled over road and field and farmyard. But we were always an island above the flood.

Between us and the railway-line the farmer had a field which dipped into a valley. The children always rolled eggs down its sloping sides at Easter. Now it was a lake. When I looked out of my window in the morning, I used to think I was still in Switzerland.

One evening the children dragged Bob's boat over from its dry-dock, perched on the high river bank, and launched it on the lake. Bob made them a sail. That evening the sky turned gold from horizon to horizon, with angry little clouds like black blotches on the sunset. I went to call the children in to bed, but just then the home-made sail filled, and the little boat suddenly took wings and drove across the gleaming water, straight into the sunset. I knew then that the wind had changed and that the long winter was over.

8

"TIMMY never comes down now," we said uneasily.

He turned up unexpectedly one week-end when the spring was making up for time lost in starting late. Everything was out at once. The narcissi were treading on the heels of the daffodils; primroses queueing for attention in the grass where a few last late crocuses were still lingering. The magnolia, incapable of learning by experience, was clearly arranging to blossom before the frosts were over, and having her usual moment of staggering beauty cut off in its prime.

Timmy told us that he had decided to resign altogether from our combined scheme for living. He gave a lot of reasons, each one sillier than the last.

"I don't feel I shall be able to stand the children now that you say you're having another and there'll be four of them," he complained.

"But you never minded the first three at all," we argued.

"I know, but the first three are getting bigger now," he grumbled.

The truth was that the ties forged in war-time were weakening among us all. We had supposed that they were permanent, but of course they were not, any more than the ties among comrades-in-arms which dwindle down, at length, to an annual meal eaten together. In this new post-war world, where there were no rations to share with each other and quarrel about, the relationship on which we had built our dream of the manor had completely withered away.

Timmy went, saying he would send for his furniture when he got a flat of his own.

We did sums and faced the fact that we could not support the manor on five-sixths of her previous income.

We decided not to tackle the problem until after the new baby was born. Two new residents joining the party at once would be confusing.

One midsummer Saturday evening there was thunder in the air. It had been hot and dry for weeks and weeks. The roses were parched and limp and the borders grey and colourless with the drought.

Diana and I felt so hemmed in, among the bare, dry lawns, that we went for a walk through the village—a thing we seldom did.

On the other side of the village hill was the Moated Grange, which had recently been surrendered by the War Office. The villagers avoided it, because it had been requisitioned, during the war, by a Bomb Disposal Unit, and everyone for miles round believed that the bomb disposers, when in light-hearted mood, used to pitch unexploded bombs into the moat and run off in fits of laughter.

Diana and I leaned over the gate and looked at the green water and the grey house beyond it.

"So it's really empty at last," said Diana. "I wonder what sort of a mess it's in, inside and out."

"It must have been lovely once," I said. "Howard told me there was a walled herb-garden and a panelled study opening into it and a hall that the Haberdashers' Company built."

Diana could hardly tear herself away.

"I often wish I was married and was mistress of a place of my own," she said. "I'd like to give up the stage and raise children and bottle my own fruit and invite my own guests."

You could hardly breathe that evening. It got dark strangely early for midsummer. The birds seemed uneasy and every now and then there would be a twittering from the dark shrubbery. The owl flew as usual, but silently, not hooting at all. An inexplicable depression hung over us all.

At two o'clock, the sky split open and there was the biggest crash since the blitz. It was no use counting the seconds between lightning and thunder and saying that the result equalled the number of miles securely between oneself and the storm because, according to that calculation, the storm was right in the garden. The noise and the blinding flashes woke the children, who could sleep through any storm in the ordinary way. When I passed by the west windows, on my way back from the nursery, and saw the village church on the hill silhouetted, like an apparition, against the black darkness, and reeled back as the crash came, I thought it would wake the dead that lay in the churchyard there. It became increasingly clear that it was going to wake the unborn. I rang the doctor and heard his voice distorted and patchy, like a broken gramophone record. I went around the house, collecting the things I needed. I thought then, as I still think, that it is sheer madness to spend the hours of giving birth in a drab and impersonal nursing-home. Having a baby is the biggest drama at which you are ever likely to be present, and the one at which you definitely have a ring-side seat. You know that this is the most important moment of your life, and the one and only reason why nature bothered to produce you at all, and it is a sheer waste to spend it in a sterilized bed surrounded by the soothing utterances of bored nurses. This time, I told myself gleefully, I had a setting worthy of the event.

I went down to the store to collect the things I had left there, and to the kitchen to make a cup of tea. Now I was in a mood of intense excitement, I was delighted with the storm. It rolled around the garden, gathering strength for great chords of noise. As I went through the hall, it appeared before me in black and dazzling white and then vanished again. I wondered how many women, over the hundreds of years during which the manor had been a family house, had been in my own case, in the summer midnight. I wondered how many of them had clutched the smooth carved wood of the banister-rail and clung to it, as labour began. I wondered how many babies since the time of Elizabeth the First had first seen the sun rise over the old tree at the top of the lawn, and whether it would be struck by lightning tonight. The house felt safe and alive and comforting. The atmosphere of a place that has been lived in for a very long time is something real and almost solid. Your forerunners do leave an impression upon it, which you never get in a newly-built house. Tonight I was very conscious of it. It seemed as if all the perished people once housed here would have told me, if they could, that all crises pass by in the end.

The dawn came up, as it only can when there has been rain after a long summer drought. I could smell the wet lilacs and the dripping, refreshed roses outside my window. The doctor went home through the lanes shining with wet leaves.

The nurse took the baby away to share the Magnolia Room with her. I didn't want to sleep. I listened to the birds celebrating the passing of the rain and watched the sun come up. Now my relationship with the manor was finally scaled. However many houses you have in your life, you are bound, by a deep and indissoluble bond to one in which your baby was born.

Morris sent in the best raspberries and roses every day; Howard built a wire-netting cage, with a gate in it, for the baby's pram, so that he could lie anywhere in the garden without fear of marauding cats or snakes. Diana sang the baby all the songs out of *Lisbon Story*, so that to this day when I hear "Pedro the Fisherman" I remember that long, hot summer and the faces of Jane and Colin and the old baby as they hung over the baby-basket and looked, with critical attention at their latest brother. The baby liked the songs immensely, but it made Diana still more dissatisfied with her own arrangements.

Diana and Bob and Lefty had been vaguely attached to each other since quite early in the war. We couldn't even remember, by now, whether Lefty had first taken her from Bob, or Bob from Lefty. We could only remember that the switch-over had been extremely trying for everyone around them. Since then, they had settled down to a routine change of shift, which appeared to hurt nobody.

We knew well enough that if two of the party married, nothing would ever go so smoothly again. When you have lived in a mixed and overcrowded household for six years of war, you learn that two married couples in a house always form two opposing camps, possibly because they talk things over in bed. But it was clear that our household was heading for change. The ring in the Christmas pudding, which had found its way into Diana's portion, had evidently known just what it was about.

On the whole, we hoped it would be Bob. Lefty was inclined to be bossy if he got the chance, and he and Diana united might be an indigestible ingredient in our mixture. Bob, on the other hand, never quarrelled with anybody. It was not that he was never annoyed by the rest of us, but because the time needed to discuss the point at issue took him away from things he wanted to do.

However, it was decided in favour of Lefty. Bob consoled himself by turning the grooms' rooms, next door to the stables, into a carpenter's shop and disappeared down there permanently, only returning to the house for meals.

When Lefty and Diana spoke of the future, they spoke of staying exactly as they were, except that they would share the immense East Room, with the copper beech outside the window, and the carved oak fireplace with Dutch tiles, where, as they pointed out, they could boil a kettle for their morning tea.

One morning, Lefty went into the ironmonger's in the market town for a pot of paint. It was the lunch-hour and the only person behind the counter was a fellow in tweeds with a handlebar moustache. "I know nothing—but *nothing*—about pots of paint and things like that," said the handlebar moustache, in a very R.A.F. accent.

He and Lefty got talking, while they waited for some menial to appear and get the paint. His name was Geronwy Jones and he was going to set up a gun-smith department for the ironmonger.

Geronwy sold Lefty a gun, and Lefty forgot all about the paint, but brought the gun home and shot a squirrel in the garden, which made us all very indignant. We liked having the squirrels so close to the house, and the corpse looked like a broken toy. Lefty said that they were vermin, and that if they had not got tails we should never have given them a second glance.

Geronwy was new to Kent and homesick for his native Wales. He took to coming over to the manor to try out new guns in the garden. We begged him to stick to the rooks and leave the squirrels alone. Sometimes he and Lefty shot rabbits and sometimes the thieving wood-pigeons and sometimes clay pigeons. I seemed always to be locking the children safely in the barn until the cease-fire.

Geronwy had one peculiarity. Women gave him asthma. He was allergic to them, as some asthmatics are allergic to cats. If there was one in the room he began to choke and suffocate and either he or the female had to go home. This meant that Diana could never be included in any of their shooting parties, and even had to keep at a safe distance when they sat sipping mugs of cider together in the garden.

Geronwy naturally knew everyone who shot, for miles around, and he used to get Lefty included in his invitations to shoot. Sometimes they went up on the Downs and lay in wet ditches, with camouflage over them, waiting for wild duck. Geronwy was incredibly hardy, and could lie with the rain soaking him from above and the wet ditch from below, all day long without so much as a sneeze. But the moment he got close either to Diana or to me, he was helpless. He didn't dislike either of us. But he just could not venture any proximity. Diana began to get silent and stayed nights in London quite often.

The farmers began to ask Lefty and Geronwy to come round and clear rabbits and pigeons from their fields. At first we thought that pigeon-pie sounded like something delicious out of a Scott novel. That was before we tasted it.

We had pigeon-pie hot and cold, stewed pigeon—which was particularly nauseating—and stuffed pigeons on toast, which looked fine until you tasted it. We made a week-end feature of having cold pigeon for breakfast. Visitors always cooed with delight the first time. None of us could bear to confess to Lefty the truth about the pigeons, because he always came in so modestly triumphant, with half a dozen of them dangling from one hand and his new gun from the other. "That'll settle your meat problems for a day or two," he would say kindly. There was only one occasion when I really welcomed the pigeons and that was when they had been stealing Morris's seed-peas. Morris was irritated about it, because planting out peas is a long and tiresome job, and I was irritated because the seed-peas had cost quite a lot. Lefty and Geronwy built themselves a hide-out at the bottom of the vegetable-strip by the river and picked off the thieves, one by one, as they sneaked down to the bed. When I cleaned the pigeons I found their gorges full of the peas, just swallowed. I collected them all and gave them back to Morris, who put them back in the pea-bed again and put wire over them. The next lot of pigeons had gorges full of the grain I had recently bought for the hens. I took it down to the hen-yard and returned it to them. But next week, the pigeons had got under Morris's wire and were full of seed-peas again, and I had to return those all over again. It made a lot of work for everybody.

We decided that the only way to stop the flow of pigeons into the larder was to get Lefty and Geronwy interested in some other creature, and began to talk wistfully of rabbit-pie. But if there is a protein more tasteless than pigeon, it is rabbit. We had rabbit-pasty, stewed rabbit, roast stuffed rabbit and rabbit stripped of bones and lying in a white sauce masquerading as left-over chicken.

When the farmer cut his big cornfield he invited any of us who liked a bit of fun to go over and watch the last stage of the cutting. The harvester swept round in a smaller and smaller circle, like a Red Indian siege. Presently one or two rabbits made a desperate dash for safety, and were picked off with guns. All the farm-hands and a whole lot of men from the village were on the side-lines and they began to cheer and jump about as though it was the climax of some great sporting event. When the island refuge got so small that even the rabbit-brains registered it was unsafe, they made a combined bid just as if they knew that it offered the only chance of escape for one or two of them. The bystanders went into fits of laughter, and cheered and tried to catch them with their hands. Lefty and Geronwy opened fire with a continuous rat-tat, like machine-guns, and the farmer hit a rabbit on the head with his stick and collapsed with mirth. I went indoors, wishing very much that I could have bread and cheese for supper.

Lefty brought the rabbits in and laid them in a row on the kitchen table. They looked exactly like the last, sad picture in a Beatrix Potter story with a tragic ending.

Next time I was in the ironmonger's, I called to Geronwy, from a safe distance across the shop, to ask if we could not have a change from vermin for once. He was stung and invited Lefty to accompany him on a very select shoot at the Priory home of the proprietor of the *Kent Messenger*. I knew they had a keeper and bred pheasants and I looked up game recipes all day, and even made an orange salad which would do even if they only got some wild duck. They came in late. They said they had had a very good day and shot an immense number of pheasants between them. Our share of the bag was eight rabbits.

Lefty and Geronwy were getting so handy with their sporting rifles that they started to look for new worlds to conquer. Geronwy was sent to a sale, by the ironmonger, with instructions to pick up any sporting rifles that were going cheap. But the sale was at a house which had mouldered into deserted silence gradually, as the manor did before the war, and there were no rifles among the lots. Instead, there were some old muzzle-loading guns which had been stuck up on the walls of the house since the middle of last century. He bought those instead and gave one to Lefty. After that, they scorned modern guns entirely and made a collection of muzzle-loaders. It looked more like the props for a second-rate costume drama than anything else, but Geronwy and Lefty hung over it as if it had been Ming pottery. They used the guns, too. It was agony to see them pack the rusty muzzles with gunpowder and ram it down with a ramrod and then fire it off with a joyful, questioning expression, wondering if it would explode and blow them to pieces.

Experts from all over the country used to come and see their collection. They were always being described in the *Shooting Times* or else writing letters to it themselves, saying that it was unsporting to use modern rifles as they did not give the game a chance. The muzzle-loaders certainly did. We returned to eating butcher's meat or our own bacon.

The news-film men came down and took pictures of them, and they were on television, complete with their decrepit weapons, in *Country Magazine*.

"I can't understand it," said the farmer blankly. "It isn't as if cartridges were as dear as all that. I could give them a tip about getting them cheap, anyway," he added hopefully. He missed the sweep of slaughter they used to make of the vermin around his fields. With the muzzle-loaders, it was a good day when they got a sitting rabbit.

One day they packed their muzzle-loaders and gunpowder in Geronwy's old car and said they were going down to the marshes by the sea for the day. I was mildly interested because, if they should happen to blow anything to pieces, it might at least be wild duck. They were so late that I began to wonder if one of them had been the victim at last. I heard Geronwy's car stop at the door. Then, to my horror there was a sliding, bumping noise. Somebody was dragging something heavy and dead over the gravel.

Geronwy and Lefty came into the light of the porch lamp, with what appeared to be a dead ostrich in tow.

"We got a swan," they said.

"You have to give it to the King," I said cautiously. It was going to look overpowering in the larder.

They said it was a Whooper and that only mute swans were Royal property.

None of our cookery books made any mention of cooking swans. In despair we made a paste of flour and water and covered the swan with it, so that it looked like an impressionistic statue of a symbolic bird. We crammed it in the oven and roasted it for the whole of the day, from morning till night. Then we had a grand dinner-party by candlelight. There is no doubt that a swan adds distinction to a meal. Geronwy developed a bad attack of asthma through sitting next to Diana and had to go home. He was very nice about it. It was Diana who was angry.

Next week-end she brought a new friend down; He had a handsome profile, a racing-car and an Alsatian bitch in the back of it. He never stopped talking, from Saturday to Monday, and whatever subject came up, it turned out that he knew all about it. He turned up for lunch an hour late and seemed surprised we had started without him. He thought everyone knew he never lunched until half-past two on Sundays. We spent most of the week-end sitting in Lefty's room among the muzzle-loaders because if we sat in any of the downstairs looms he would find us and relate stories about himself. His name was Dirk.

Diana seemed discouraged by our silence when she talked admiringly of him, and a week or two later, brought down a substitute. He was a Scottish vet. He was completely speechless from arrival until departure, but we agreed he was at least an improvement. However, he ruined the good impression on the last evening of his visit. We were sitting in the drawing-room, trying to think of conversational topics, when he suddenly took a pair of pincers out of his pocket and took out two of the dog Doubtful's teeth, without a word. We were more indignant than the dog, who, indeed, seemed more surprised than angry. We protested afterwards to Diana, but she said very coldly that it was very nice of him not to charge us a fee.

Two weeks later, Diana broke it to us that she was going to get married. Dirk was the prospective bridegroom.

"Of course, we don't really know him yet," we faltered without much hope.

Dirk had been married before, and had two boys whom he brought down for the week-end. Both of them could have gone straight into a case-book of problem children. The only things they really enjoyed were breaking the other children's toys, having fights with them and bringing tales to us.

"You will feel all right about Dirk taking Timmy's place, won't you?" Diana asked us anxiously. "And the children can be brought up with your children. It will be good for them all," she added generously.

There was one ray of hope. We waited for Dirk to realize that Diana had been in love with Lefty, before the muzzle-loaders came between them, when he would almost certainly stamp and swear and say that he would not live in the same house as Lefty.

That week-end we decided to cut down a tree which was suspended dangerously over the road. Howard said that if it fell on the head of a passer-by, the Council would make us support his widow and children for the rest of their lives.

My husband took Howard's great axe and swung it and brought it down, not on the tree-root, but on his foot and collapsed under the tree, not merely bleeding, but spouting blood. It was one of those moments when you merely stand still and stare, because you believe that nothing quite so awful could really be happening to you and that in a second your eyes will focus and you will find it was a hallucination.

Lefty's war, however, had been spent in the little ships of the Channel, where they all doubled for gunner, engineer and doctor all the time. Without our own moment of frozen inaction he whipped off his scarf and made a tourniquet, bandaged the foot up with a handkerchief and his tie and then looked round as if surprised to find himself in his present surroundings. The ambulance backed down among the undergrowth and Lefty, still looking as if he was in another world, picked up one end of the stretcher and sat down beside us in the back.

At the hospital there was an Irish house-surgeon with a brogue so thick that any conversation between us and him was a dead loss.

Howard unlocked one of his mysterious sheds and produced a bath-chair. My husband sat in it, on the lawn, and thought about being lame for life. The foot turned green, and we brushed up our Irish brogue and went back to the hospital to complain. We were defeated by finding a Chinese house-surgeon on duty. So far as we could make out he was telling us there was nothing to be done about the green foot and we might as well go quietly home.

Our doctor was away on holiday.

"Don't say nothing," said Howard. "But you never ought to have gone to that hospital. Didn't you know there were two? If you pick the wrong one, the doctors tell you that now you've made your bed you must lie on it."

It was Lefty who discovered an army doctor and brought him home. He unpacked his kit on the lawn, having forgotten that civilians are tended indoors. The foot turned from green to blue and back to skin-colour. One thing emerged from that week's wear and tear. We could not possibly spare Lefty from our household. If it came to a choice, he must be the one to stay.

"Dirk won't live in the same house as Lefty," said Diana.

"That's what we thought," we agreed.

I missed Diana terribly. When she forgot to think and talk about love, she was the gayest and most congenial companion. It was mournful too, that another foundation member of the scheme had resigned. We began to feel nervous about the future.

Diana was homesick for green fields. One afternoon she rang up from London.

"Dirk and I have decided to take the Moated Grange," she said.

They set up an exact copy of our *ménage*. They got a German script-writer and his wife to share the Grange with them, and Dirk's mother moved in, with his two children. She was to act as chaperone for Dirk and Diana until they were married. In her own sphere, she was a first-class character actress, and she put on the best performance as a tweedy countrywoman that I ever saw in my life. She made all the real ones, for miles around, look phoney, including the Colonel's daughter.

Sometimes Diana called to see us when Dirk was away. He would not visit the manor, nor allow her to with his knowledge, because of Lefty. Diana was full of high hopes that she and Dirk were going to settle down to an orderly, idyllic country life, just as we all had been when we first moved into the manor.

One day, when I was helping Noel to bottle the damsons, she said, "The Moated Grange is empty again."

Her boy had seen the furniture-vans coming out of it, on his way home from work. We went up that evening to see if it was true. The Grange was as empty as it had been the day Diana and I first looked over the gate. We wrote to her and she telephoned us from London.

"We just got out before we went bankrupt," she said. She added that now the party had broken up she had decided not to marry Dirk after all. She thought she would marry someone quite different. We tried to be attentive and interested, but her tale of the financial crisis had struck us more than the emotional one. "Our turn next," we said.

9

THE lilacs were dripping wet in the garden, the day that Howard died. A few days before, his old wife, who never stirred from the tiny garden around their cottage, had trudged up to the house to ask me to telephone for the doctor. He came and was not hopeful.

Twice every day I called at the cottage to ask how he was.

I would hear her slow, heavy footsteps painfully descending the narrow stairs. When she at last reached the door and opened it, she was speechless and panting for breath. One day I could not bear to fetch her struggling down again, and decided that my inquiry was more trouble to her than it was worth. I got as far as the stableyard and turned back. Howard died that evening.

"He kept on asking for you," the old wife said without reproach. "I said—'She's sure to call in to inquire, like she always does, and then I'll ask her if she'll kindly step upstairs for a chat.'"

Even at this distance of time, I remember the lilacs heavy with rain and the cuckoo calling mournfully, as I went back, up through the garden. It taught me one lesson for life—when in doubt, always make your gesture. The risk of being a nuisance is the lesser one.

Morris helped to carry the coffin down and out to the waiting hearse.

Howard had left orders that he was not on any account to be buried in the village churchyard. We had to drive a long way, to a cemetery the other side of the market town. It was an impersonal place, and the flowers were meagre and commonplace. We put some of everything that was blooming in the manor garden on Howard's grave.

Afterwards, so long as we were at the manor, I kept on coming across pieces of work that still lasted on, although the hand that wrought them was decayed. The garden forgot him in one season. Nettles grew in the places he had cleared. Ground-elder strangled the border where he had never allowed it to intrude. The great dahlia he had planted outside the dining-room window, so that we could admire it as we ate, bloomed and withered and was gone. The roses he had pruned so strictly reverted to barbarism and produced too many lanky and weedy blooms.

But the fence that he had put up against the rabbits stayed strong and effective. The gate he had mended swung sweetly, with never a squeak. As I stood at it one evening, calling the children to bed, I noticed how each screw of each hinge had been set in with the most accurate and meticulous care. I remembered how Howard had once told me that when he was a tiny child, his brother had locked him into a coffin-like box and he had been rescued by his mother with only seconds to spare. What had he done with the sixty years she had snatched for him? He had served a tradition through its very last decade. He had tried to set it going again, teaching us the ways of the manor. And we were not going to survive, after all. His dedication to the house had reaped nothing; and the garden had blotted out all traces of his conscientious hand. Only these material things survived; the sturdy wheelbarrow; the carpenter's bench; the new spade-handle; the fence; the mended gate. So far as I know, they must be lasting still.

Howard's married daughter took over. She drew down the blinds in the cottage windows and communicated with us by little notes. At last the keys came to us, silently, pushed through the letter-box. We did not know until then that Howard's old wife had gone.

I wondered if she had thought of the day she first came, a raw kitchen-maid of fifteen. She must have walked up the back drive meekly and fearfully, carrying her modest bag made of straw; for, fifty years ago a new kitchen-maid was very small fry indeed. Did she remember, as she went, the triumphant years when she had ruled the great house and kitchen-maids had trembled before her? Her crab-apple jelly was famous for miles around, and she never divulged the secret of the artichoke soup which was peculiar to the household. Even today the immense strip of vegetable garden given up entirely to artichokes is a memorial to her skill. But she went out as she had come in, furtively, down the back drive, fearful of prying eyes from the windows of the house.

We let the cottage to friends from London, who furnished it, sparsely and beautifully, with antique furniture. They polished the floors and put Persian rugs on them. They had a sofa with faded brocade and pale linen curtains and a harpsichord with keys like ivory silk. But I missed the overcrowded ornaments and the upright piano, with a picture of the Colonel on horseback, and the curtains of Nottingham lace and the little box with shells glued all round a mirror, marked "A present from Hastings".

One morning I turned the tap on and got a whistling sound instead of water. I automatically turned towards the door to go and consult Howard before I remembered that Howard was dead.

I asked Morris, who replied that the same thing had happened in his cottage and that his wife was not pleased about it.

"But didn't Howard tell you anything about the water?"

"Only about the sewage," said Morris.

We had our own sewage plant half-way across the field—a horrid mystery which none of us cared to examine.

The agent said that after Howard's death he had arranged for the village garage-man to look after our water-supply. The garage-man was impatient and said we should probably have some water tomorrow. We did, and were lulled into a sense of false security. But when you are born and bred supposing that taps contain water as a natural thing, you dismiss any failure from your mind as a mere freak.

After several unexplained dry days, we discovered that our water came from a spring on the hill beyond the garage. The Colonel's father had tapped it, installed a ram-pump with a paraffin-engine and laid pipes across the fields to the manor.

I learned to start every bundle of the baby's washing uneasily, and if any one of us had a bath he did it secretly, knowing that he would be unpopular if there was no tea for breakfast. When we had no water, the cottages had none either. The weekending Londoners, in Howard's old cottage, used to come up to the house and beg for a cupful. They always suspected that we had a secret jug of it, hidden away somewhere. It was true. But I guarded it jealously for the baby's porridge.

"Try the river," I used to advise them, standing guard over the locked cupboard containing my private store.

The river was a blessing. We could at least wash up. We had to eat vegetables raw, or else bake them in the oven with dripping. As the cold weather came, the house began to feel damp and chilly, because there were so many days when we could not have the boiler.

One day the garage-man told us we should not be having water for the next ten days. We appealed to the agent.

"It seems there's a part missing off the paraffin-engine," he said. "Howard had some way of patching it up, but Wragge can't find out the dodge. He's going to the factory in

Lincolnshire where the engine was first made to see if he can replace it."

We put a trunk call through.

"Can you give us the number of this engine?" asked a voice from Lincolnshire. When I gave the date, which was 1879, I thought I heard a ghostly chuckle, over the two hundred miles of wire. Maybe it was the ghost of Howard.

"We don't seem to have any of those in stock just now," said the factory manager politely.

"Now we're further off getting it fixed than ever," Wragge grumbled. "I wish you'd leave it to me."

"You've got Mid-Kent water at your house," we said crossly.

Eventually he remembered that he had a brother-in-law in Birmingham who had a workshop and decided to go up there and make a new part with the assistance of his relatives. He was hurt that we did not greet this solution with gratitude.

"We shall have to go and stay somewhere until you get the pump going," we said hopelessly.

But where? When you have four children, including a young baby, your friends do not clamour to put you up for ten days. A hotel was out of the question. Running the manor without Timmy or Diana was making our bank accounts look very sickly. Since Howard's death, we had been paying out money for gangs of men to do repairs once done by his cunning hand alone. We stayed where we were.

The men of the household went off to work unshaven and bought cups of tea in the station refreshment-room. My husband's department of the B.B.C. was at that time installed in the Langham Hotel and one of the hotel bathrooms was still left untouched, next to his office. He took up razor and soap and towels, sneaking in past the commissionaires every morning with his coat-collar turned up to disguise the fact that he was fresh—so to speak—from getting out of bed.

I got complaints from the school about Jane's neck being dirty. I washed the baby's clothes in the river. The whole of every twenty-four hours was dominated by having no water.

"I want to know what they did here in 1878," said Bob. "They must have had water of some sort."

Mollie's young man from the village said that his old father had heard there was a well, but he could not remember hearing whereabouts on the four acres it was. This piece of information threw us into the frenzy of wilting desert-dwellers up against a mirage. It was agonizing to know that there was water somewhere on the premises. It might be only a few feet from where we were sitting now. If only Howard's ghost would come back, how willingly we would give him the freedom of the manor in return for the one piece of information we needed!

"Is there a spiritualist in the house?" we wondered.

There was the next-best thing.

"I never mentioned I was a water-diviner," Morris confessed modestly.

He promised to find a forked twig and start the minute the daylight came back next morning.

But that night I dreamed that the cistern was full, and, like the Ancient Mariner, when I awoke it rained. The rain seemed to be drumming unusually loudly and we discovered that it was leaking through on to our bedroom floor. This was too good to miss. We leaped up and collected basins and jugs and went round the house looking for leaks under which to place them. There were six or seven altogether. Howard had always looked after the old roof and seen to getting it patched up. No one else even knew which trap-doors and skylights led to which part of it. At the moment, even more leaks would have been welcome. It was wonderful to have water without having to go out of the house for it. Morris came up from his cottage through the downpour, to explain that the conditions were not favourable for water-divining.

It rained for days. We scrubbed floors and washed our hair. We took turns to get up in the night to remove filled vessels from under the leaks and replace them with empties. The fields flooded, but we had no patience with the farmer's troubles. When a patch of blue sky showed, it was greeted with frowns and grumbling. "It isn't much," we said hopefully. "Probably the clouds will swallow it up again in half an hour." But they didn't. When we heard one or two birds strike up, we knew that our brief holiday from drought was over.

The fields were under water still. Bob borrowed Lefty's bicycle and went up to the spring on the hill, hoping for signs of life. Wragge should have been back by now. But the two little huts which held our private reservoir were locked and barred, with sacks hung over the windows inside. Bob poked about and peered through keyholes, and decided that the only job the Colonel's paraffin-engine had to do was to pump the water from its spring into its tank. After that it simply flowed under the fields to the manor.

We went into Ashford, to the coaching-inn. Our ostensible object was to have a drink; our real one to slip upstairs, in turn, and have a secret wash, in warm water, in one of the residents' bathrooms. While the rest of us sat, prolonging our drinks, to give everyone a chance, we stared out of the window at the closed doors of the fire-station, hoping that the engine would dash out to add some human interest to the scene.

"Firemen must be simply idling about this weather," said Lefty, severely, in his war-time voice.

"That gives me an idea," said Bob.

We all trooped over to the fire-station and demanded to see the chief.

"If our house should go on fire," we said to him. "Your men would fix their hoses to the fire-hydrants, wouldn't they?"

He agreed cautiously.

"Nothing would happen," we said. "There's no water on the premises at all." He was new to the district and did not know about the river. We told him the history of our water-system, since 1879. He was interested, but not as disturbed as we should have wished.

"I don't understand why you're telling me all this, you know," he said amiably.

We wondered, if his men were bored and idle, whether they might not find it a diversion to drive a fire-engine up the hill to the spring and hose water out of it into the tank. He did not jump at the idea. He said it was irregular. It was only when I mentioned the baby's washing that he began to get interested.

"We've got a baby that age at home," he said. "I'll see what I can do."

When we were having lunch, there came a sound as welcome as the pipes at Lucknow—the fire-engine charging up the road to the hill beyond the village. We remembered that the two huts were locked.

"Firemen break down doors as a matter of course," said Lefty consolingly.

As it turned out, they did not have to. Wragge had returned. When a helmeted head peeped into his ramshackle garage, he was alarmed, and surrendered his keys without a murmur.

"It seems almost incredible that I shall turn the taps on and water will come out," I said dreamily. But the taps gave back their usual hollow whistle and not a drop of liquid. We telephoned Wragge, who was surly.

"I'm trying to do the best I can for *everybody*," he said. "I had to give the village people a chance to get their cisterns filled first."

"The village is on Mid-Kent water."

"Oh no it isn't," said Wragge. "Only some of the cottages. The cottages that used to be part of the manor estate are on the manor supply."

Almost speechless with rage, we telephoned the agent.

"I believe there are some of the original manor cottages drawing from your tank," he admitted. "But I have no idea which ones, nor how many. None of them belong to the manor now. If you'd asked me a year ago, of course, I could have asked Howard."

"Naturally you'll never find out," said the policeman. "The ones that are on your system don't have to pay a water-rate, because you pay for the whole service, such as it is. I suppose the manor always has done and always will."

"Not while we have the strength left to stop a cheque," we said.

We invaded the garage in a body and told Wragge that if he did not switch the water from the village cisterns to ours, within twenty minutes, we were going to refuse to pay the quarterly sum we sent the agent, which was then sent on to him as a reward for his struggles with the pump. At that Wragge agreed to go up to the spring and turn the water into the manor pipes.

Next morning, as soon as I woke, I ran to the bathroom and turned the tap on. It moaned and whistled and did not yield a drop.

"I tell you I had the supply switched to you all night long," said Wragge. "I shan't be able to look the people around me in the face if they get to know—specially considering that all that the firemen pumped up is finished now."

"If he's speaking the truth, there must be a leak in the pipe somewhere," said Bob.

We stood on the river bridge and looked across the fields to the hillside. There was a mile of fields between us and our spring. It was impossible that the pipe should lie in a straight line, because our sewage-bed was in the way. But we had absolutely no idea what course it plotted.

"Howard knew it, every step of the way," said Morris. "I've seen him going zig-zag over the field, when he wanted to stop a leak. He was going to show me how the water-system worked, so that I could take it over after him. But we left it till I got settled in, and after that. . . ." He stopped, and looked sheepish. After that, they had never spoken to each other again, and Howard had carried his secret to the grave.

The fields still lay below water.

"When they dry up, I'll take my hazel-twig and find out the course of the pipe for you," Morris suggested consolingly. "Once they're dry, we shall be able to see the leak bubble up from underground," said Bob.

Even the farmer was not more anxious than we were, for the flooded fields to clear. We led a curious, uneasy existence, like an absurd dream, in which we waded through deep puddles to the bus, came in soaked from the garden, but had no water indoors. We heard, with the remote lack of interest with which a prisoner in a dungeon might learn it was spring, that Wragge had got the paraffin-engine fixed up and that the water was running merrily down the pipes to the village.

But one morning we woke to find Morris calling below our window.

"I've found it!" he said. "I could feel there was a drying wind last night and I went out first thing with my hazel-twig. But I didn't need it. The water's bubbling up through the ground. I left the twig to mark the spot."

Bob and Lefty and Morris and Wragge dug all morning and located the break. We had to ask a local firm for a piece of new pipe and they had to send to London for it. However, eventually there came a day when I met Colin carrying a cupful of water to put beside his bed.

"Where did you get that?" I asked him.

"Out of the bathroom tap," said Colin matter-of-factly.

But from then on, we never knew security. Any hour of any day we would find the taps dry. Looking back, I remembered that Howard had often disappeared, mysteriously, after warning me to say nothing and not to be alarmed, as there would be water for all before long. I remembered, too, his mysterious remark about having refused the manor to the Brigadier's wife because she had talked about putting in an extra bathroom. That mystery at least was resolved.

10

LEFTY'S firm sent him to the Far East. He was divided between regret at leaving the manor and exultation at having a chance to see the world. He packed his muzzle-loaders away in his cupboard and reminded us that Geronwy would be lonely and should be invited over to shoot the pigeons from time to time.

Geronwy was bereft. One morning some trigger-happy Amazons spent an hour looking over sporting rifles in the shop. Geronwy went home and lay on his bed, in the little hut where he lived alone and cooked his own meals, gasping with asthma. He felt so terrible that he made his will and left his half of the muzzle-loaders collection to Lefty. Next day he came over and deposited some bottles of wine in our cellar. They were to be kept there until Lefty's return. He himself, he added, revelling in Celtic gloom, did not expect to be spared to see it.

Now we had to support the manor on half our original income.

If you have a house three times too big for you, it ought to be possible to shut up two-thirds of it. There was only one way we could have done this with the manor—by moving ourselves into the servants' quarters and staying there. No group of people could support themselves in any other part of the house. In our long struggle with the manor, she always defeated us because she had been built as a gentleman's residence. The north wing, holding the kitchens, was the engine-house of the great building. And the engine-house had been deliberately placed as far as possible from the gentry's quarters. If you wanted to keep a log-fire to warm yourself in the drawing-room, the most southerly point of the building, and also to keep in the boiler—the most northerly—you would not be able to sit by either. It would mean, instead, a continual journey to and fro—through the hall, through the great dining-hall, down the kitchen passage, and back again, round the other side of the square, along the west corridor, past the preserving-room and the store and the wine-cellars, though the double doors which led into the back hall, and through the second double-doors into the front hall again. Yet, so long as Noel and Mollie lived at one end of the manor and we lived at the other, the house fell harmoniously in with the scheme, because it was a very modest and simplified version of the scheme for which it had been built. They lived their own cheerful and cosy life, punctuated by shrieks and giggles which we never heard, in one wing, and kept the machine running, while we lived in bare and spacious simplicity in the other. It was a most agreeable plan for all concerned, if only it had cost a little less.

"Or if only we could make the manor subscribe a little bit towards her own upkeep," we fretted.

But she was an aristocratic lady on our hands. All ideas for making her work for a living were wrecked on the fact that she was born to be served and not to serve.

We surveyed our four acres of ground and thought that we ought to be able to make money on them.

It was the standard town-dweller's dream of country life and just as fantastic as the country girl's idea that if she goes to live in the city she. will find her fortune. Everyone who moves into the country pictures himself planting seeds out in the balmy spring weather, and the money chinking into his pockets at harvest-time. It is true that you ought to be able to reap some pin-money from four acres, and if the manor had stood in a four-acre field, perhaps we might have done. But she stood in a pleasure-garden of lawns and herbaceous borders, and vistas planned to look enchanting from the windows. Her kitchen-garden, orchards and vegetable-strips were planned in order to keep the squire's table supplied from January to December. We called in a neighbouring market-gardener to advise us. After two hours of wandering disconsolately round the gardens, he came back to the house and said:

"I'm sorry—it's impossible. There isn't one single long, broad stretch of ground on which you could grow enough of one crop to pay for getting it to market. You simply cannot make any kind of a living from this garden. You can only be supported by it yourselves."

It was irritating that the people in cottages and council-houses made themselves a few shillings weekly, in the season, by taking tomatoes and beans and bunches of flowers in to market. But these things were extras, above what they needed for themselves, and as their small plots were kept entirely in their own spare time, they had no overheads to pay. All the same, we did try sending one or two good cabbages, a straw chip full of currants and a box full of lettuces, from time to time. When we had paid the carrier's charge, and the auctioneer's fee, there was rarely more than half a crown left for us. Our wages bill for the garden alone was seven pounds a week.

We had two orchards and it seemed to us, with memories of London fruit-shops, that we might get some profit from them. But if you want to sell apples in Kent they have got to be round, symmetrical, and all of a size and texture. Our orchards were full of trees that looked like a fairy-tale—as though they would walk away, waving their twisted arms, when the moon was full. They were perfect to sit in or climb. What they should have been was about four feet high and monotonously skinny and straight. A money-making orchard, compared with an old orchard that is part of your garden is like a class of flat-chested little schoolgirls in rows, compared with a roomful of glamorous women. When we sent our apples to market, they left us with a deficit, because, beside the carrier's fee and the auctioneers, we had had to employ paid labour to help us pick them all in one day. Our only clear profit was when we "sold a tree". A man with a lorry, some ladders and two mates came round and selected the best tree in the whole garden and paid us four pounds down for all the fruit on it. He picked it and took it away himself.

But we could not make ends meet. However much we tried to eliminate luxuries, we were paying for the most expensive luxury of all—privacy, space—our own piece of land. We might eat boiled cod and parsnips, and wear ragged clothes. But we woke, between our patched sheets, in large lofty rooms, with the sun blazing through great mullioned windows.On the wide grass stretches, enclosed from the road by ancient trees, our own footprints would be the only ones in the dew. And our children's life was stripped of everything cheap and harmful and full of everything that is right for childhood. We were willing to do without everything else; but even so we could not pay for these things.

There was Colin's education to think of, too. Although he could climb like a monkey, swim and paddle a boat single-handed against the stream, hit a bullseye at fifty yards with an air-rifle and turn a herd of hysterical cows out of the garden without letting them trample the roses, he had still got to learn to read and write. We were depressed at the thought of taking him away from his free, outdoor life and shutting him up in the little village school, with its over-crowded classroom and enclosed strip of asphalt which served as a playground. We knew we ought to give the manor up, and one spring evening we went to bed with our minds made up.

It was cold, and we got into bed rapidly and silently and lay staring into the darkness and listening to the farm dog, three fields away, baying the moon.

When we awoke, it had snowed. On the wide stone balcony outside our window, it lay thin and white on the balustrade. We went out in our dressing-gowns, and found an unbelievable sight. I have never seen anything like it since and I suppose I never shall again.

All the early summer flowers were covered with snow. The wistaria had each hanging bunch of purple gleaming through the white. The pink lilac looked wine-coloured beneath it; and the white lilac had turned cream against its dazzling texture. The last yellow daffodils sprinkled the white flowerbeds with gold. The primroses were buried. Only a faint edge of pink or yellow showed here and there, as though they were a glimpse of coloured parcels buried in some celestial bran-tub. We stood above the garden, not feeling the cold—remembering the old legend about the virtuous girl who found strawberries growing under the snow.

"It's no use," we said, as we went indoors to dress. "We can't leave the manor."

That evening we took pencil and paper again, though we knew the figures by heart now. Six of us had been able to support the manor comfortably. Three of us were using the same space, the same heating and the same minimum of service. If we had added the first three again, it would have made no difference to the house itself—only to the bills.

"Suppose we tried to turn it into a guest-house?" we suggested. There was a guest-house in the next village. Noel knew one of the girls who worked in it. When she came, one day that week, to have tea with Noel, we asked her about it. The answer was discouraging. There were only one or two very old people as guests, and they had to be waited on hand

and foot. Even so, the owner could not manage to keep it going and was making arrangements to close it down.

Then a Dutch impresario who had just brought the B.B.C. Symphony Orchestra safely back from a tour of Holland came down to the manor for the week-end to recover from the nervous strain. Her everyday existence was exactly the life most housewives dream of, as they peel potatoes and darn socks. She flew between one capital and another as casually as we take our shopping bus. She knew world-famous hotels as we know the shops on our regular shopping round. But she fell in love with the manor from the first morning she woke in the deep silence just before dawn, and watched the magnolia flowers emerge into daylight as the dawn chorus began. It worried her to think of all the time she had wasted staring at Swiss mountains and the monotonous indigo of the Cote d'Azur. No one, it seemed, had ever told her about Kent.

She was an agreeable mixture of sophistication and sound Dutch common sense and we confided our difficulties to her.

"But of course," she said. "You must take foreign tourists. I will put some advertisements in foreign papers for you and even if your terms are modest, you'll be able to make quite a lot of money."

When she got home, she cabled from the Hague to say that two Dutch typists would be arriving next week to spend their annual holiday in the Garden of England.

It was great fun, getting ready for the tourists. We spring-cleaned the guest-rooms and put carefully-chosen books by the bedside—*Peter Rabbit* and *What Katy Did*, as light reading suitable for beginners in English, and all the maps of Kent and bus time-tables we could find. We drew up advertisements for the French and Swedish papers—French because we were so handy for the Channel ports, and Swedish because they had hard currency and were allowed to spend it. We cleaned out the boat, ready for boating tourists, and decided that we ought to get the court ready for tennis.

The nets and posts in the local sports shop were so expensive that it looked as if the tourists' profit would be eaten up before they even arrived.

"There must be some dodge for doing it cheaply," said Bob.

He bought some old Radar equipment at an army sale—tall metal masts—and erected them round the court. He went to Rye and bargained with the fishermen for old herring-nets. They smelt deliciously of tar and were still strong enough to stop a tennis-ball if not a draught of fishes. The court was very bumpy, but one of us always rushed to roll it the moment there had been a shower of rain. Fortunately, the tourists all turned out to be rabbits.

We instructed Morris that we should need more daily vegetables and apples from the store. He brightened up immensely. The morale of the manor's personnel was always low when she was not running to capacity. Morris undertook to supply any quantity required and even volunteered to grow mustard-and-cress in the greenhouse to make sandwiches for the tourists' teas. This really touched us. Every professional gardener regards mustard and cress as a task too low even for his garden boy.

Noel and Mollie had not the slightest objection to our filling the house with tourists. Over this kind of thing, we reaped the advantage of our new forty-hour week in the kitchen. They knew that if they worked longer than usual they would get more. Therefore we were in the strong position of not having to feel apologetic towards the staff because we asked someone to stay in our house. Noel and Mollie reaped the reward of their broad-mindedness about the tourists in the tips they got from each party in turn. Also they got a lot of entertainment in the kitchen that summer, giggling over the fact that foreigners couldn't speak English like everyone else.

The tourists visited Canterbury Cathedral and the Cinque ports and sat under the magnolia tree writing postcards home and made halting conversation at meals about the British way of life. By the end of the fortnight, we were shocked to discover ourselves becoming more and more picturesquely British. They were so wisely amused when we argued about cricket, that it seemed only kind to make their evening by continuing it. We felt morally obliged to eat roast beef and Yorkshire pudding, even when the mutton at the butcher's was better. Even when their visit was marred by icy winds and rain, they were painstakingly pleased, because it corresponded with all they had learnt about the British summer. Their favourite bit of English life however was marmalade. They bought jars of it as souvenirs to take home to their friends.

Our next tourist was a Swedish widow. She touched all our hearts from the first day, when we discovered that England was her dream-country. In her little city flat, like a thousand others when she got up in the dark mornings of the northern winter, she told herself stories of England which she had never seen. In England the winds were sweet and mild. Spring came early and the darkness was short. In England, flowers that cost a kroner each in Stockholm grew in the hedges for all to pick. In England, a merry informality, replaced the stiffness and cold manners of Sweden. She collected pictures of the British Royal Family. She went to the cinema only when British films were shown. In the long lonely evenings she taught herself English and founded an English club in her small town. She saved up for a long time for her first holiday in England.

She arrived at the manor, bewildered by walking into her dream at last, on the very morning when the magnolia burst into bloom. With her, we had no need to put on a painstaking act of the British Home Shown to Foreign Tourists. She assumed that everything we did was wonderful, and so we could afford to be ourselves.

The first evening it was chilly and Mollie lit the kindling under the logs in the hall. We pulled up the chairs and turned to her. A sweet smile broke over her face.

"So you really do it?"

We were startled.

"It says in the books that when the English light one of their open fires they pull the chairs up and sit in a half-circle round it. I always wondered if that was correct."

One evening she came into the garden while Colin and the farmer's boy were having a boxing lesson from an ex-army instructor.

"I understand," she said. "In England, even the little boys are so kind that they have to be taught to fight each other. In Sweden they do it without being told."

She loved to hear someone tell a long, painstakingly funny story brought back from the village pub. She never could follow the story. It was the reception she waited for.

"So the English really do laugh out loud when friends are together," she would say contentedly.

We supplied her with *The Edwardians* to read in the evenings, explaining the phrases to her when she got stuck. Then we sent her off, with a packet of sandwiches to spend the day at Knole, telling her it was Chevron House, in which the book was set. We awaited her return with sympathetic interest. She came in and looked at us speechlessly.

"It's too much," she said at last. "It was too beautiful, and too large. I'm going straight to bed."

The day before she left she went round digging up daisy-roots and violets and primroses from the hedge-bottom.

"I shall put them in pots and have an English green-house in my flat. Do you think they will bloom?" she asked anxiously.

She went off with her bag laden with souvenirs and with the diary she had kept of her visit, in English, which we had all corrected every evening like a school exercise.

"Another satisfied customer," we said, as we mournfully watched her train out of sight.

The next tourist was a Swedish poet. He sat by the river writing a poem about it. Otherwise, he was not fond of water. He liked the house and Kentish scenery but could not accept Kentish cider as a serious drink. He thought it was supplied for the children and waited anxiously for the hard liquor to appear.

We never had spirits in the house. If we supplied him with whisky and gin, it was not only going to cancel any profit from his stay but leave us in the red for his living expenses. So we took to keeping out of his way whenever we saw the thirsty light in his eye, which was often. One morning, shortly after breakfast, he desperately stopped Colin in the passage.

"For the love of heaven, boy, get me a drink," he pleaded. "And not that soft sweet stuff out of a barrel, whatever happens."

Colin, who was used to being sent for cider, went into the wine-cellar and looked round. All he could see, besides raspberry vinegar, were the bottles Geronwy laid down there, against Lefty's return. They were home-made country wines—parsnip and wheat and elderberry. Colin selected the nearest bottle, which was wheat wine, and poured it into a cider-mug and took it to the Swede, who tipped it down his throat. "Got any more?" he asked, handing the mug back.

We could not make out what had happened to him that morning. The Scandinavian melancholy was not evident at all. He drank up all of the home-made wines before he left, and said they were the best hard drink he had found in England and better than what he got at home. At his earnest insistence, we shared a bottle with him in the evening before he left. It tasted like the concoctions the children bought at the village shop, but knocked us practically unconscious. Next morning we had the kind of heads which suggested we had been drinking whisky and gin all night in some smoky dive. The Swede had no hang-over at all. He finished the last bottle before he left to catch the breakfast-train.

*

June brought the beginning of the French school holidays and an invasion of French children. Their parents, immensely impressed by the photographs of the manor, which we used to include in our answers to inquiries, supposed that their children were going to stay with the lesser nobility. The children appeared to be relieved when they arrived and found it not like that in the least. Some of them were having a last holiday before an arranged marriage. But that did not prevent them from playing cache-cache, with passionate enthusiasm all day in the garden. The big boys played tree-climbing as seriously as if it had been mountaineering, negotiating a single tree the whole morning and then sitting thoughtfully at the top of it, planning how to get down.

They joined the class which was held for Colin's benefit in the garden every morning. We had solved the problem of getting him educated without imprisoning him indoors by collecting a group of boys the same age to do lessons with him. They sat at long trestle tables on the terrace with their books and chalks and counting-frames before them. When Mollie took out their elevenses, three or four chaffinches, who had been hanging about waiting for it since dawn, flew down and joined the party. They sat on the children's shoulders, grabbed their biscuits and took sips from their milk. When the French children joined in the lessons, for the sake of their English, their shrieks and giggles alarmed the chaffinches immensely. Colin and his companions were so used to the birds that they paid very little attention to them, except to insist on having some part of their biscuits themselves. But the French children went into daily hysterics. After a bit, the chaffinches got used to it and took no further notice.

They never stopped talking, for sixteen hours a day, as none of them ever went to bed before ten o'clock at the earliest. If you stopped to listen to the prattle, it would be some absurd triviality, being discussed with so much vigour that it made you feel fatigued just to listen. They thought we were utterly brutal and unloving when we requested our own children to stop talking or to leave us alone to be quiet. We came to the conclusion that French married couples must embark on raising a family because they like to hear children prattling, just as people buy a canary because they like to hear it sing and twitter.

Sometimes, when we got a new consignment over from France, and looked at them, sitting all down both sides of the long refectory table, and remembered that they were going to be there for every single meal for the next few weeks, and on our hands all the hours in between, we used to wonder if we could face it. Sometimes I would get in a kind of panic and think wildly of telling them it had all been a mistake and they were to go back to France by the next boat. Then I would go upstairs to my own housewife-of-the-manor quarters. There I had my own room and the nurseries and a special room for sewing and ironing. The ample cupboards held winter clothes stored away. The house-linen was neatly ranged on shelves. The sewing-machine stood always ready for use. Another set of shelves had cottons and scissors and patterns, and the week's mending. Never, before or since, have I been able to keep the household machinery in such beautiful order. Below the window of my little linen-room, Morris had planted a lavender-hedge for me, all round the little courtyard. I kept the bunches hanging to dry in my sewing-room and then put the dried blossoms in bags among the sheets. All summer, whenever I sewed or ironed or sorted linen, the scent of lavender came floating in from the courtyard. The humming of the bees in the lavender hedge was like the murmur of a mill-wheel that never stops. When I was alone up there I would know that I would willingly entertain the whole of the United Nations all the year round if it would enable us to keep the manor.

The French children went home, to take part in the family holiday which followed the educational one, with their vocabulary much improved, if not their accent. They had learned to call each other "clot" and "big-head" and to refer to any female who displeased them as "that old cow". Colin could switch to broken English—which they comprehended far better than the intact article—without a second's pause. Jane had been so startled to discover that the language she was painfully acquiring at school was actually spoken by ordinary human beings that she developed a passion for French which has lasted her ever since.

After the French children, we had a German one who was ingenuous and charming, an American one who was neither, and after that several Finns, some adult and some not. The Finns were sad and withdrawn, much given to brooding silently over grievances which, when examined, all boiled down to the fact that the English were such a *dirty* race. Then we had a tall, ugly Swiss girl who had the most electrifying effect on all the men for miles around. She had a dark gamin face, like Leslie Caron, and she walked like a goddess. If she went into the garden, Morris and the boy would turn as red as the peonies beside them. If she went to the market-town, the wolf-whistles all down the street used to sound like a flute symphony. The agent sent some men to paint the window-frames, and after the first day they simply abandoned any pretence of work and followed her round with their paint-brushes in their hands, looking hypnotized. She herself was completely wedded to the intellectual life. She spoke six languages fluently and spent all day reading abstruse books and discussing philosophy with anyone free to listen. She would not speak sharply to the tormenting painters because she said it was not ethical to snub a poor man. All August and September the sun blazed and the lawns turned yellow and Bob had to invent an irrigation system, based on the river, for the vegetable garden. The Swiss goddess was saddened because she had wanted to see the original of the expression "English grass"—that is, grass which is particularly tall and juicy through constant moisture. Also, she kept on hoping against hope, till the day she left, to experience a pea-soup fog, such as she had read about in Dickens.

After her, we had a French girl, from a sheltered provincial home.

She was afraid of bees and wasps and shivered if the ants scuttled about near her, when she sat in the garden. She could not even bear the thought of mice, and one evening, when one was wandering about the house, she threw hysterics when she met it. But she had been in the Maquis during the war, and had twice jumped by parachute to give instructions to isolated units, broken her leg in one jump and twice been arrested by the Gestapo. Once we took the children for a picnic to the sea. She looked out of the train window and remarked that one little country station put her in the mind of a village in France where the station-master had been a *collaborateur*. Her group had been tipped off to get him out of the way. "My part was to engage him in friendly conversation and edge him down beside a truck with petrol in it," she explained.

"What then?" Colin asked.

"We threw him into it and set fire to it," she said, gently taking the baby on to her knee and beginning to play a finger-game with him.

One night we borrowed the farmer's car and took resident tourists for a moonlight picnic to see the Olympic runner hand over the torch. We sat in a little wood by the side of the Dover Road and watched the spark of light, away in the dark distance grow into a man with a flaming torch in his hand. It was a satisfying experience, as though one had expected something of the sort every still summer night, on the long straight stretch of road between London and the sea.

*

The first frosts came, and the sun had worked round away from the lawn every day by the time we finished tea. The last tourists had departed when Rafael Kubelik suddenly arrived at the manor, with his wife and child. He had been behind the Iron Curtain when we last heard from him. He had managed to get permission to bring his family with him to the Edinburgh Festival. They were not going back.

It is strange to have people under your roof at the beginning of their exile. Some mornings after their arrival they got their first letters from home after the papers had announced Rafael's decision to stay in the West. I shall never forget how they opened them and took them away silently, into the garden, nor their speechless grief all day. They would not speak of their own country or the past. Mollie and Noel discovered that it was the little boy's birthday and made him a cake, with his name on and two candles. He was delighted with it. Rafael, too, brightened up and murmured respectfully, "Ah—I understand—an English folk-custom." They were the easiest guests we ever had—carried wood upstairs to light a fire in their own room, when they wanted one, as if they had lived at the manor all their lives and fell into the day's routine without a single question. Perhaps it was because Rafael spent all his childhood wandering around the world with his father, knowing every capital of the world as most children know the parks and playgrounds of their own town. Or perhaps it was because the Kubelik family are at home both in the sophisticated atmosphere of a first night at the opera and also among the very simplest people—but not anywhere in between. They were perfectly happy helping us to store the hay and cut wood and feed the hens, and equally happy at the Edinburgh Festival, but in their life there was not—and never has been—any room for inessentials, like tray-cloths and fish-knives and music that is neither primitive nor classical.

Sometimes they took the early train to London, cheerful as a gipsy family on the march again, and returned by the last one. I would find them, at midnight, sitting round the kitchen table, eating bacon and eggs or spaghetti, talking and laughing in animated good-humour. I used to wonder, as I went up to bed through the sleeping house, whether the ghosts of the Flemish weavers listened, catching, in the laughter, the homesickness beneath, remembering how this same roof had sheltered them in just such a flight and just such an exile.

11

THE first gales of winter swept the trees clean of dead leaves, and carried the sea-gulls inland. They spread over the ploughed field so that, from a distance you got the impression that it was blooming with manna. "It's stormy at sea," we used to say. Picturing the storm which would send the gulls flying for shelter made us feel cosy, in our garden which was so thickly hedged with trees that you always got the impression the wind had dropped, when you came in the drive gate.

We had a sudden influx of tramps. Noel said she had heard in the village that our gate had been marked. We privately thought that the reason for the manor's new popularity with wayfarers was because the dog Doubtful had now abandoned all pretence of doing guard-duty for his keep, and given himself up to a life composed in equal parts of women and hunting.

Two tramps knocked at our windows one wild and stormy night. Their accent made us feel as if the tourist season was still in full swing. They produced wallets thick with papers, proving that they were in England on a potato-harvesting permit. The other papers were permits to help with various harvests from Lapland to the Mediterranean. We had never realized before that you could be a tramp on a proper international basis. They appeared to think that the British permit entitled them to stay with us for the night, so, as any conversation between us was a waste of time, on account of their knowing no English, we put them in the Magnolia Room. Next morning, they sawed up as much wood as they considered equal to a night's lodging and departed.

Our next tramp was an Italian Duchess. She had come over, with her car, on the night-ferry, and been sick all night long. Fifteen miles inland, the pangs of hunger began to gnaw at her unpadded vitals, and she remembered hearing, from the child of a Parisian friend, that we kept open house at the manor. She drove in at the gate and demanded breakfast.

The next tramp had an Oxford accent but his conversation was purest Bloomsbury. He was obviously delighted with himself, standing outside the French window and begging for a meal, and longing to be asked why he was doing it. Eventually he was driven to announcing, "I'm just out of prison."

I began to clear the table as a hint to him to hurry.

"Don't you want to know what I was in for?"

"Not specially. Do you want any cheese?"

"I was a con man. We're by way of being the intelligentsia in any prison. I could always get away with it with housewives, you know. They get so bored and frustrated that they'll let any man in."

This stung me into describing how the last uninvited guests but one had sawed up a whole pile of logs as a mark of gratitude, and adding that there were still plenty waiting to be done, and he took himself off in dudgeon.

Then there was the soldier who stood next to me on the milk-train one night when I had been in London and missed the theatre-train. He had his three-year-old daughter sitting on his kit-bag. She dropped off to sleep and rolled off it so often that I suggested they got off with me at Ashford and spent what was left of the night at the manor. We had to walk home. All the way along the dark muddy road, he kept on telling me how his wife had skipped with another man just before he arrived on leave. He was not so much shocked by her unfaithfulness or her deserting the child, as by her selling the sideboard to pay for her elopement. The child never stirred in her sleep when we put her to bed in the Magnolia Room, but he sat up all night writing a poem to his wife. The refrain of each verse was "You sold our sideboard". Mollie and Noel took a copy each, and he gave the original to me, and went off saying he was going to present the little girl to the sergeant when he got back to camp.

Then there was the afternoon I still do not care to remember, when Noel reported that there was a soldier asking for a cup of tea. We always kept my mother's rule about never refusing food and drink at the back door. She had held that it was better to risk a cup of tea on the most barefaced impostor than to be caught out at the Last Trump. Mollie and Noel had not the slightest objection, since the callers were usually soldiers. Noel suggested offering him the cold sausages and I went into the garden to fetch the baby from his pram and Morris came racing up to me:

"You know who's in the kitchen?" he said. "It's the Mad Parson. He's the image of his picture in the papers. They said he was letting on to be a soldier."

I went into the kitchen and there was a shifty-looking character with his eye on the door, I thought of telephoning the police, but the telephone was in the kitchen passage, which made it embarrassing. I beckoned Noel out of the kitchen and pushed the baby into her arms and bundled them both into the drawing-room and locked the shutters and the door and took the key away. At that moment, the postman arrived with the afternoon post. I told him to dump the letters on the kitchen dresser and come back and tell me who was sitting in there. When he came back he said:

"It's the Mad Parson."

"You'd better ask the first policeman you see if he's interested," I suggested doubtfully.

It was only minutes later that I heard the police car. The two occupants behaved so like police in films that we seemed to have shifted into a different, nightmarish world. They slipped into the kitchen and stood one each side of him before he could rise to his feet.

I knew then, when I saw the sick fear on his face, that he was not the Mad Parson, but that he was on the run. They searched him, with his hands above his head and took his small secrets from him, and went away. I was so ashamed, I could not look him in the face. I gave him some clothes and some shoes and enough money to catch a long-distance bus. He was a deserter from the army. I didn't ask why. I knew I should remember all my life that I had asked him into the house, offered him hospitality and then secretly betrayed him. Noel had tired of the drawing-room and broken the shutters open and taken the baby to gossip with Morris in the garden. "It's all very well," Morris argued, when I told him. "But you've got to think of my position. If your husband came back and found you with your throat cut, he'd have a right to ask me what I thought he paid a man to stay on the place for."

When the half-yearly bills came in, we got a fright. The tourist profits had lulled us into a false security. We began to realize that the seaside landladies who blame the short holiday season for all their troubles were not so far wrong. It was all very well to make the manor support herself from June till September. There was all the rest of the year when we were legally bound to support her and could not do it.

We gave up everything—cakes, cigarettes, cider, sending linen to the laundry and clothes to the cleaners. We practically gave up eating. Anyway we had no appetite.

We had been brought up in households where bills were paid weekly and where, if they were not all disposed of by Saturday night, everyone went around looking as if the police were after them, until Monday morning. When we got a curt demand for the manor's immense rates, and knew we had not enough in the bank to meet it, we were both frightened and terribly ashamed.

I sat in the little waiting-room outside the Bank Manager's office and rehearsed my opening speech.

The Bank Manager was startled, but sympathetic. He asked for the whole story and looked perplexed when I described how we had planned it all in the fear and darkness of the air-raid shelter and emerged into the sunny orchards of Kent. At the end he said, "There's only one solution. You must give up this house."

"Give up the manor?"

"Yes, of course. You could live perfectly well on your income anywhere else."

He had got interested in the problem now, and sat thinking it over.

"When I get a case like this," he said, as if people in love with Tudor manors dropped into his office every day, "I always ask myself—now what should I do in their place? Now I know what I should do in yours. There's a little house vacant in the road by the station, with a little yard at the back where your children could play. Why don't you inquire about that?"

We knew his advice was good and that we should have to take it. But it would be turning the dagger to live so near to the manor. We should have to take the children for country walks, eternally, and the road led straight by the manor gates All we needed was an angel with a flaming sword on duty at the end of the drive.

We went, instead, to look at little houses in Tunbridge Wells. But there were only big ones, with prices to match. In despair, we viewed a house which the owner had divided into halves, so that she could let one. She inquired closely into the habits of our children. It was clear that from now on our family life would consist of alternate sessions of apologizing for the children to her, and for her to the children.

I lay in bed, saying to myself, "We only want half a house, half a house. Where can we find half a house?" At three o'clock I suddenly sat up in bed and said aloud:

"Fool! You've got a house that's twice as big as you want."

I did not even bother to try to sleep after that. I was far too excited. I stayed awake until the birds began to tune up, planning it all out. A house with four wings falls easily into two separate halves. The servants' bathroom would serve one half. The flower-room, with an electric cooker in it, would make a kitchenette. We could take a housemaid's pantry each. One group would use the back-stairs and one the front. There would be no more division of the household into below-stairs and above. Those days were finished for ever. From now on it would be divided vertically, into tenants and sub-tenants.

When morning came, I woke the others and told them we were saved. They listened, with the dawning recognition with which you always welcome a plan so simple and so obvious that you cannot imagine how you overlooked it before.

We interviewed the agent, and he telephoned the Trustees. They agreed without a murmur. Next day we got a letter from one of them, in a fine scholarly old hand, dwelling regretfully on the unavoidable difficulties that beset people like ourselves and him with a Labour government in power.

In the best traditions of squirearchy fallen on evil days we interviewed our dependants and told them we could no longer afford their wages. In the best tradition, they instantly offered to work without any and were relieved at our refusal. Mollie and Noel had both been planning to get married that summer anyway, and merely told their young men that the date was now put forward to Easter. (They married, and moved in with their in-laws, decided to wait for a baby until they got a house; then, after much fruitless waiting, to have a baby in order to get moved up on the housing list. Long afterwards they did, in fact, reach the top. They installed the babies in expensive prams and brought them down to the manor to be admired. They both continued to look cheerful and efficient and could be picked out, at a hundred paces, from the other village mothers because they were well-groomed about the head and feet. So far as I know, they both lived happily ever after, as they richly deserved to.)

We arranged that Morris should keep his cottage, and potter about the garden, evenings and week-ends, by way of rent, but take a daily job to feed his family. We asked the Council if they needed a gardener in the town parks. Their enthusiasm startled us. Within a fortnight, Morris had been promoted from labourer to head park-keeper, with a forty-hour week, overtime pay and a guaranteed pension. He never ceased to lament his previous job with us, and drew unfavourable comparisons between the timid approach of the Parks Committee to him and our own (correct) high-handed way of complaining if everything in the garden was not as it should be. Also, he became more and more firmly Conservative, feeling that putting him in charge of labourers, when he would rather do the work himself, was a typical piece of left-wing tyranny.

But it was the ninepence-in-the-shilling boy who reaped the most surprising harvest from the manor's downfall.

He got a job with the Catchment Board men, who, from time to time took possession of our territory while we meekly stood by, like Chinese peasants invaded by bandits, hoping that they would go away before, they finally ruined our piece of land. The Catchment Board paid him, above his wages, "discomfort money" for standing about in the river. Whenever I saw him, up to his thighs in water, dreamily poking about for bits of water-weed, he looked completely happy and fulfilled, and as if he had found his niche at last. He made six or seven pounds a week, of which he paid his mother one pound and put the rest away in the post-office. His status in the village changed completely. The girls stopped mocking him, and began to look at him thoughtfully, but he paid no attention to them and went on putting his money away. He must be a warm man by now.

12

NOW we were on our own. The garden seemed empty, without Morris and the boy. The kitchen wing was like a tomb, without Mollie and Noel.

I called on the kind Bank Manager and told him our plan for letting half the house.

"I can find you a tenant," he said at once. "A client from the army camp, who wants to have his family with him. He asked me again only this morning if I knew of anything. I'll send him round this afternoon."

That afternoon, the Major called. He was a nice little red-faced man, in charge of the electrical arrangements of the unit. We learned from him that it is wise to avoid living on the same circuit as any top expert electrician. So long as he was in the manor, it was a mass of live wires and plugs without any attempt at insulation. He put in switches which you turned on from the bath, or with your other hand in the sink. You trod on sparking wires wherever you walked. Fuses blew daily and he mended them with wire so thick that every connecting one could have burned itself out before the fuse noticed. The regular electricians, whom we had to call in frequently for repairs flatly refused to go into his part of the house. They said they were much too frightened.

The Major was only frightened of his wife. He had called on the Bank Manager that day because he had received rather a stiff ultimatum from her by the morning's post. He was so relieved to be able to tell her he had found accommodation for her, that he agreed to every arrangement we suggested without a sentence of discussion. It was arranged that he should have the New Wing and the part of the garden which it overlooked. This meant that he got all the old kitchens, but had the boiler as handicap.

"That's all right," he said. "I'll bring my batman with me. Nothing these fellows like better than fugging over a fire."

We scrubbed out the Major's half of the house, ready for his wife and family. We discovered one of the catches about taking furnished tenants. You have to divide all your possessions in half, down to tea-towels and saucepans. If you keep the better ones for yourself, you are being a grasping landlady. If you don't, you are being plain silly.

On the last day before the arrival of the family, the batman brought down his camp-bed and set it up in the butler's bedroom. He sat down on it and looked round him so despondently that we were wounded. It seemed to us that he ought to be in the seventh heaven, moving from the camp into the manor, just as the daffodils were blooming. He assured us grudgingly that he had nothing against the house itself, though personally he preferred newer models. It was the thought of sharing it with the Major's wife that discouraged him.

We were a little discouraged ourselves by the Major's demeanour as the day approached which was to unite the family. He seemed more nervous than exhilarated. At the last moment he brought down some rugs from the Officers' mess and called us in to ask anxiously if we thought they made the room look more furnished. We said cheeringly that anyone who had got a Sheraton cabinet, an oak refectory table, five eighteenth-century chairs, a plaque of St. John the Evangelist, which was so valuable that it had to be insured separately, and two striped rugs from the Mess as well ought to consider herself in clover. He gave a twist to a live wire which he had recently brought up through the floor-boards and said if we could lend him an electric fire to attach to it, he thought it would give a homely air. We undertook to light a log fire instead, and to fill the room with daffodils. He went off to the station to meet her.

Our first impression was of a slightly dowdy, faded little blonde woman with three subdued children. We showed them their quarters, which they looked at in silence.

For the first few days, the boiler dominated us all. The batman could not make it go, possibly because he never raked out the ashes. The Major's wife used to send one of the subdued children to fetch us, to start it again, whenever it went out. We thought of speaking harshly to the batman, but when we heard what the Major's wife could do in that line, we realized that if she could make no impression, we were scratched at the starting-post. Also, he was so downtrodden that we were automatically ranged on his side. He had been moved out of the butler's bedroom and made to put up his camp-bed in the dreadful little scullery, with its peeling walls and stone sink.

Although the four wings of the manor had fallen neatly into two equal halves, neither was self-contained. We shared a common strip of passage, the water, the electricity and the garden. It would have been difficult for any two families to accommodate themselves to each other without trouble. It was just our luck that we had struck on the Major's wife.

She had been following the Major around the world, living in married quarters or lodgings, for twenty years, and we were the newest and greenest of lodging-house-keepers. We were wax in her hands. Within a fortnight, we had handed over the best henyard, the courtyard with its lavender hedge, two new brushes and our coal-scuttle, all the doormats, and our right to use the tennis-court and the boat at week-ends.

"This won't do," we agreed with each other. "Another month, and we shall have no more spirit left than the Major."

For the next fortnight, we opposed her on all occasions. It was not a success. We had visualized her giving way before a firm hand. We learned a fact of life which I always remember now, when I am tempted to smile contemptuously at some hen-pecked man who has got himself amusingly into the Sunday papers because he has appealed to the court to rescue him from his wife's tongue. The fact is that in order to stand up to it, you have got to dismiss the idea that a little spare-time exercise in the sport is enough. Most people only enjoy a quarrel when they are feeling in the mood. But this won't do. You must have a practice round at every opportunity, not merely when you are offered a game. I lost a lot of ground through being out of training. By the time I had had a good slanging match with her at noon, I was fit for nothing for the rest of the day. If I got involved in another before teatime, I was worn out. By eight o'clock, I was ready to give away the Magnolia tree. But she was just as fresh and fluent as she had been first thing in the morning.

A blight seemed to fall on the manor. The very children turned furtive and quarrelsome. Our beautiful geese, unwisely straying into the tenants' part of the garden, were imprisoned in an empty henyard. The batman had privately selected it as a dump, for ashes, to save himself a tiresome walk down to the rubbish-heap. He threw in some smouldering coke, and next morning the geese lay dead beneath the quince tree.

Our plan for running the manor by amateur labour began to show its weaknesses. In theory, two families could keep the garden going, with part-time help. It meant cutting out all the jobs the full-time staff used to do, which did not seem immediately necessary. One of these was the weekly sweeping of the inner courtyard. The gardener's boy used to unlock it every Saturday morning, sweep round with a broom and lock up again. We had often been amused by this traditional procedure, which never seemed to add visibly to anyone's comfort. Now we learned better.

The cobbled yard was completely enclosed, it is true. But it was open to the skies. Seeds blew over the roofs. Within a few weeks, blades of grass began to push up between the cobblestones. It looked pretty, but we thought we would weed them up later. Moss spread over the centre drain. A timid little plant put up some pale shoots at the foot of the pipe which drained the roof-gutters. Before we noticed, the drain was blocked and the water from the roof was motionless in its pipe. There was a stormy few days, and the roof-gutters filled with rain-water. Unable to get away, it flowed back over the roof, under the slates and brought down the bedroom ceiling beneath. Having the ceiling replaced cost us more than the garden-boy's wages for six months.

In the garden, convolvulus wound itself round the currant-bushes, and die birds found a gap in the raspberry-nets and appropriated the crop. Nettles presented themselves, fully fledged, in the most unlikely places. The latch of the greenhouse door, left unmended, allowed the door to swing in a high wind and all the panes of glass were smashed. We felt as if a malicious poltergeist had taken over the place, always just out of sight, so that you came upon new wreckage always in new places. And we lived in a state of guerilla warfare between the two halves of the house.

We talked of giving them a quarter's notice. But the Major's wife had so drummed into us the glaring weaknesses of the arrangement that we were perfectly convinced we should never find another tenant and that we should have to give up the manor after all. She told us that we should never find anyone else foolish enough to take on a rambling collection of cold, shabby rooms, at an exorbitant price, with ill-disciplined children (ours) running in and out of the shared doors all the time. She herself would not have considered taking them for a moment, had she been consulted. The Major, of course, was not capable of knowing a fair bargain from a shameless racket. There might be, she implied, a mug born every minute, but we could not expect to have the good fortune to run across two like the Major in one lifetime.

It was at this moment of near-despair that Mrs. Williams came into our lives. Perhaps it would be more accurate to say that she dragged us into hers. Looking back on the Williams era, I remember every detail of the fantastic jealousy and grief and violence and utter despair which raged in the kitchens. But I have completely forgotten anything we ourselves were doing at the time. The elements which made up the life of the Williams did not belong anywhere in our own lives. While they were with us, it seemed as though two different kinds of story had got mixed up in the same book-cover. In the front wing of the manor, a quiet domestic novel chugged along its tranquil way. In the back wing, there was a kind of twentieth-century *Wuthering Heights*.

But I could hardly be expected to guess that she was bringing the shadow of death to hang over the manor, when I looked up one morning, as I was gathering roses, and saw her standing at the gate looking up at the house. Several times she approached the front door and then went away again. At last she came back, walking very fast, and rang the bell. When I went up to her, she jumped violently, then looked at me and relaxed.

"I had an idea that Major's wife lived here," she said.

She was a plain, ordinary-looking middle-aged woman. Or was she? Now I know the devotion she inspired, I feel as if she should have looked striking. But all I saw was a sallow-faced, dark-haired woman in a black suit and high-heeled shoes which were not, as I judged, a perfect fit. She said she had heard I wanted a few hours' cleaning every week. I countered by asking if she wanted to clean. She replied that she had no real need to go out to work at all, but didn't mind obliging me. I answered curtly that since I proposed to pay the standard labour rate, I should not feel under the very slightest obligation to anyone taking the job. She looked at me in silence for some minutes and then said:

"You and me'll get on."

We did get on. Within a fortnight, I was under the same spell as her first husband, her second husband, her seven children, her stepdaughter and her son-in-law who was a Czech airman. He used to hang about in the sky above the manor garden, waiting for her to come out. Her fourth son, who was on the railway, used to shunt up and down the railway-line all afternoon, hoping for a wave of her hand from the lawn. Her stepdaughter spent her pocket-money on presents for her; her second husband glowered if she borrowed a trowel from Morris. Her grown-up children by her first marriage called to see her when their stepfather was at work and quarrelled with each other if she spent more time on one than another. I found myself resentful if she was busy with her family when I wanted to tell her something or consult her.

We found that we never told "my-daily-woman" anecdotes about her to our friends—those patronizing anecdotes, proving how utterly democratic you are, which have replaced the old comic-domestic-servant jokes which you find in old *Punches*. On the contrary, we found ourselves telling anecdotes about our friends' idiosyncrasies to her.

She used to hold me spellbound, over the dishes, with her tales of raising a family of seven during the years of unemployment. In the hot June sunshine, as we shook mats in the garden, she could make me feel the biting east wind over the potato-field, as she bent over her sack, looking across, with despairing anxiety, at her children, huddled in a row beneath the hedge, waiting for her to finish and take them home.

One day she went off to challenge the batman, who had scrounged one of her brushes, and took the opportunity to examine the Major's part of the house.

"If the Major was to go," she said, "You could let off that first floor of the back wing as a self-contained flat. Then you could have a strong married couple living in the kitchens, looking after the house and garden. They wouldn't need a bathroom. They could wash in that little old scullery, where the batman sleeps."

I explained that our reason for dividing up the house was because we could not afford to pay for service.

"We wouldn't want wages," she said. "We'd do it in return for the rooms. You come and call on me some Saturday and see the place we're in now."

You had to go up a grimy little alley and down some steps into the damp darkness to get there. Although it was a warm afternoon, the basement struck chill. It had been condemned long ago, but was waiting for some building programme to materialize. Holes in the plaster had been freshly repaired by Mr. Williams and painted over. Dry-rot was swept up immediately a fresh little heap of dust fell. There were flowers in a vase, neatly placed in the exact centre of little crocheted mats.

"The minute we get a chance to throw out the Major, we'll do it," I vowed.

Three weeks later, he went of his own accord. Once we began to want them to go, the wife's claws were drawn. The more she abused the arrangement the Major had made, the happier we got. We all felt, irrationally, that the battle was won the week she lost her voice. It was strange to know that she was in the house but not be able to hear her. Finally, a very subdued sub-tenant knocked at the communicating door and handed us her formal notice, adding, with a flash of her old spirit, that she had found another half-manor, some miles away, in twice as good condition, at half the price. And one Autumn evening, the Major's tilly drove away with its last load (the family, the hens and the two striped rugs from the Mess) as Mrs. Williams' husband drove in at the other gate, in a borrowed van, with the contents of the condemned basement.

Up till now, he had been merely Mrs. Williams' husband. Now he emerged as a gigantic, blackavised Celt, the strongest man physically that I ever met. As they moved their goods in, he picked up a wardrobe as if it had been an orange-box, swung it on to his shoulders and stood calmly holding it, while Mrs. Williams debated as to whereabouts in the room it should go. He trundled their ancient piano off the van and into the house single-handed. Hours after, when we went to bed, we saw him standing silent and motionless on the drive, watching the moon rise over the trees.

His daughter was a queer, thin little elf, with black eyes and pigtails and a gym-slip and blazer so tidy and well-brushed that it was hard to believe they had been kept, until now, among the peeling walls and dry-rot of her previous home.

St. Luke's Little Summer brought soft mellow sunshine and a complete stillness, over house and garden, as though the year had been arrested, for a moment, before it chilled and darkened into winter. The happiness of having a home fit for human beings to live in glowed like a flame in the kitchen wing and seemed to spread through the house. The Williams were a family in love, and their exultation was catching. They were in love with the solid walls and the daylight of their new dwelling-place, with the sunlight streaming in the great windows and their own garden beyond their own back door. We made over the walled kitchen garden, which surrounded the kitchen wing, entirely to them, and locked the outside gate of it and gave them the key. Within the first month, they had the ground cleared and ready to plant. But inside their flat they never stopped working. When we went to bed, their lights would still be on, and a furious sound of scrubbing, whitewashing and hammering still proceeding. Long before we were up in the morning, the kitchen would have come to life again, with Mr. Williams digging before he went to work, Mrs. Williams scrubbing and the little girl feeding the rabbits they had installed in the woodshed. When we woke, the first thing we remembered was the transformation into astonished happiness of the three down at the end of the kitchen passage.

The speed at which they made over the old kitchen wing into a flat was remarkable. They had it newly-painted, from end to end, before a fortnight was up. But the crown of the achievement was in turning the dreadful little scullery into a bathroom. Mr. Williams picked up a bath, hand-basin and lavatory at some inexplicable government-stock sale. Within a few days he had torn out the old sink and copper, replastered the walls and painted them, installed the plumbing and put lino on the stone floor. I shall never forget going down to the kitchen wing to confer with Mrs. Williams and seeing him emerge from his first hot bath. His dark face was shining, between soap and pleasure. His clean shirt was carefully left open at the neck, to exhibit the spotless skin beneath. He held himself like a king, and, for the first time, looked me squarely in the face. Now we were equals at last. And now, I thought gladly, the slavery of the little scullery-maid was paid off.

Next time I went to market, I called on one of the estate-agents and told him we had a self-contained first-floor flat to let. I was prepared for languid interest, but the avarice in his face, as he snatched at paper and pencil, startled me. He undertook to send half a dozen clients off his waiting-list that afternoon, but asked if he might look at it himself first, as he was badly in need of a place like that for his wife and family. On my way home, it struck me that it was going to be a strange bargain, since I was expected to pay him back ten per cent of his first year's rent, as commission to himself for finding me a tenant. I cancelled the arrangement and put a three-and-sixpenny advertisement in the local paper. By the time I had opened the first two hundred answers I was thankful that I had given only a box number and not the address.

On Mrs. Williams' advice we picked the couple who had been longest without a home, and who had a child at the same destructive and quarrelsome age as our own youngest. That gave us, she pointed out, two good weapons against tenant trouble. They would not lightly risk being homeless again, and would have their hands tied, in the matter of complaints against our children, by having a hostage to fortune of their own. We were awed by this masterly scheme and followed it scrupulously.

A great peace descended on the manor. The Williams snatched back house and garden from the brink of decay. They cleaned and plastered and painted; weeded and built up walls and fences, dug and hoed and cut the grass; clipped the ivy, pruned the raspberries and had the baby to tea in their kitchen any afternoon he liked, cramming him with chips and baked beans and hanging on every word he babbled with incredulous admiration. The three families in the house and two in the cottages slipped into a communal life—doing errands for each other in the town and reciprocal baby-minding. For the second time, we thought we had the manor tamed and clipped to fit in with a new scheme of living of our own.

Mrs. Williams had a visitor. When I opened the door, I thought it was a witch, left over from the Middle Ages. I took her round to the kitchen flat and presently Mrs. Williams brought me round a cup of tea out of her teapot.

"It's my mother," she said. "Can I show her round the house?"

Her mother was a layer-out of corpses. Shortly afterwards, Mrs. Williams took the afternoon off to go with her to a funeral and came back looking uneasy. She said her mum had carried on alarmingly because the driver had brought them back from the cemetery the same way he had driven there. If you were so reckless as to do that, instead of prudently throwing the unseen powers off your trail by taking a different route, they would come for one of you next. There had only been herself and her mother in the ill-advised car.

However, three days later, I heard that one of the employees of the local taxi-firm had died suddenly.

"That's right," said Mrs. Williams, surprised at my commenting on so obvious a fact, "It's the one that drove us to that funeral. Didn't I tell you about it?"

I hoped that Mrs. Williams would not make a habit of entertaining her relatives at the manor. They had a disturbing aura, like characters out of a Hardy novel.

Mrs. Williams said that all her life she had dreamed of living in the manor, just as we had. But in her case, she had known the house itself since she was a child, and had stolen daffodils from the back drive so regularly that she had come to look upon it as a right. She had answered my advertisement on an impulse, merely because of the address. Now that she was actually installed there, she liked to go over the beginning of the story over and over again. "It seems as if it was *meant*, doesn't it?" she said, respectfully referring to a Providence with a fool-proof filing system. I like to remember that she had some months of incredulous happiness there before the blow fell.

One Friday evening she came round to see us looking important. "Will you keep an eye on the boiler tomorrow?" she said. "We're going to Maidstone for our new furniture." They had been saving up for it ever since they came. They all three dressed in their best clothes and went off on the first bus. When they came back, Mrs. Williams told us we were all invited to a celebration in their flat the day the new furniture was installed. They were going to kill a chicken.

It was a pleasure to go into the Williams' part of the house. Everything smelt of distemper and paint and plaster. The new suite smelt of varnish and Rexine. Mrs. Williams gave us a round-by-round description of her battle with the salesman about letting them have it at a special price. It should have been a happy occasion. It had been a happy occasion, in a way, as we all agreed when we went up to bed. But all the same, we were glad to get away. If Mrs. Williams spoke to anyone else, her husband and her stepdaughter broke off their own conversations and listened, intensely, their heads turning back and forward like a kitten watching a blind-cord swing. If she had a private joke with one of us, they turned sulky. Bob said broodingly that he wouldn't be the man who made a pass at Mrs. Williams for the whole of his life-insurance money, in cash and tax-free.

The postman delivered an envelope with a foreign stamp. I took it round to the kitchen wing.

"From Dick," said Mrs. Williams, with pleasure. Dick was her youngest and favourite child, by her first marriage. He was serving as a boy in the navy. But when she read the postcard her face clouded.

"They're flying him home to hospital," she said. "I wonder what's the matter."

Two weeks later she was summoned to see him. When she came back she sat staring at the table.

He had an incurable cancer. The doctors said he had not less than three months but not more than a year. He was seventeen.

"The doctor said to have him home and make a fuss of him," said Mrs. Williams. She raised her head and looked at the clean paint and the fireplace and the coloured calendar hung on the wall.

"I've got this place to bring him to," she said.

Dick was brought in an ambulance from the Naval Hospital. The men who unloaded him in the garden looked round them wonderingly. "Nice little place you got here, matey," they said. Mrs. Williams picked daffodils and gave them a bunch each and thanked them for transporting Dick, and turned upon them her own peculiar sardonic charm. Every male creature who came to the house felt it, and the tradesmen used to hang about hoping for the chance of badinage with her, long after they had delivered the goods.

She acted as if Dick had been brought back as a convalescent. We had all agreed to support the same fiction, that he was to be invalided out of the navy and to have a holiday on sick pay before taking up another career.

Dick was a tall, handsome boy with the mild, sweet-tempered expression which you often find stamped upon the face of the youngest child of a large family. In the state of life where children are an unmixed blessing, the youngest is valued because there will be no more where he came from. In Mrs. Williams' circle, the last baby received an equally enthusiastic welcome because it marked the end of child-bearing.

It would have been impossible not to take to Dick. As it was, we all had to guard against making too much of him. We kept up the bright patter supposed to be the right facade to put up against the certainty of death.

"You ought to be teaching yourself a job, Dick. Think the navy's going to support you like a gentleman indefinitely?"

"Always been bone-idle," said his mother. "He only joined up because he thought he'd have to go out and do a job of work if he didn't."

We clubbed together and bought Dick lamp-shade wires and parchment and a book on how to make lamp-shades. When he had made them, we coerced week-end visitors into buying them. Mrs. Williams had a better idea. She bought leather and tools and started him on mending shoes. "Always hoped one of my children would be a snob," she said. "There's money in it."

Dick was easily bored and would not stick to his last. He sat in the kitchen listening to the radio or in the garden reading *Real Life Confessions* and *True Horror Stories*. He began to get the look of patience which you only see on the faces of children who suffer continuous pain. From time to time, the ambulance whirled him back to the hospital for examination. On those days we always hoped, absurdly, that the surgeons would uncover a ray of hope. We all collected stories of people who had lived to laugh at the doctors' prophecies.

A faint air of cheerfulness dawned on the house when Dick collected a girl-friend. Not one of us was capable of considering her point of view.

"'He wants to do a bit of courting and he's going to do a bit of courting," said Mrs. Williams grimly.

Dick's girl was a shy little teenager from the village. One day, as they sat entwined in the pictures, she whispered:

"Dick?"

"Yes, ducks?"

"Is it true what they say about you in the village?"

"What?"

"That you're going to die?"

"Is it true?" Dick asked his mother.

Beneath her scornful denials, he read the truth.

From then on, he wasted no more time. He drew his savings out of the post-office. Each day he went off to the town. He saw each twice-weekly film at each of the two cinemas and the other two days of the week saw the more exciting ones again. In the evenings, he joined the companions of his school-days, standing about at street-corners with them or at a pin-table saloon. Often he missed the last bus home and came roaring up the drive in a taxi, long after we were in bed.

The naval ambulance still came regularly and took him away for a day.

"I want to know what's the matter with me," Dick said. "I mean to find out, too. Somebody knows. Why not me?"

"Don't talk so silly," said his mother. "Those smart doctors don't know themselves. That's why they're keeping so damn quiet about it, not to expose their ignorance. When you get better, they'll make out they knew you were going to all the time."

Dick had a buddy who was one of the hospital orderlies. Somehow he got the man to sneak his file of papers.

"I know now," he said, when the ambulance-men had brought him back. We looked at him speechlessly.

"What's all the fuss about?" asked Dick. "Why did you all have to hold out on me? Here I've been afraid all this time that it was T.B. I'd got and that I was going to die the way Dad did. Why couldn't you have told me it was cancer? I don't seem to feel the same way about that at all."

"Don't you want to get the vicar or someone to call?" we asked Mrs. Williams. She looked blank and said she set no store by parsons. One of them had been forward enough to ask why Jenny did not go to Sunday-school. She made an exception in favour of the naval chaplain at the hospital who, she admitted handsomely, had made no attempt to talk religion to her.

Jenny began to get thin and pale. When Mrs. Williams took Dick off for the day to the seaside, she was left behind with us. On those days she would not play or eat her meals. Often she spent them in what Mrs. Williams called her "Welsh mood", refusing to speak or hold any communication with the rest of us at all. Every time the bus passed by she listened, tense, to see if it would stop at the gate. Williams was not taken on these expeditions either. It was understood that he was going to spend the day working in the garden. Instead, he spent it wandering aimlessly about, drifting towards the gate whenever a bus was due.

We were afraid. We felt as if a fire was smouldering in the kitchen wing which was soon going to envelop us all.

*

One evening Mrs. Williams suddenly appeared in the study, white-faced and trembling. The cigarette I gave her shook so much that I could hardly light it.

"Dick?" I ventured.

She shook her head. Dick was at the pictures. She calmed down after a moment and said she had come round to borrow cigarettes. She didn't want to go up to the pub for them, because her husband always created so if she had a joke with the men in the bar. Her first husband had been just the same. She added:

"Dick hated him too. All the boys hated their dad."

"Do you mean Dick hates Mr. Williams?"

"Why, he'd like to kill him," said Mrs. Williams, surprised at my simplicity.

"But your husband's been so kind to him, since he was brought home."

"He knows what I'd do if he laid a finger on Dick," said Mrs. Williams matter-of-factly. I asked nervously if it wouldn't be better if we tried to get Dick into a convalescent home or perhaps to stay with his married sister for a while. She answered flatly that she was going to see him through to the end whatever happened. She absently took another cigarette and lit it from the end of the first one and observed irrelevantly that her first marriage had sorted itself out nicely when the boys grew big enough to knock their father down, and that one of them had once absent-mindedly given Williams a black eye, forgetting that he was not a blood relation. I tried to picture the life that was going on, so close to us, behind the red-baize door which Williams had found in an outhouse and put up in the passage to cut off the kitchen wing.

"Couldn't Jenny go away for a bit?" I asked at last.

Mrs. Williams looked startled, as though she was trying to remember who Jenny was, then said there was nowhere for her to go. She took half my cigarettes and went away, saying she would replace them when she went shopping next day. She was always scrupulous about returning them.

Mrs. Williams took to going to the pictures in the evening. On those evenings we used to see the dark figure of Williams behind the bushes at the drive gate, waiting to see the bus stop. If she got off, he would shrink back into the bushes, through the orchard and round to the back door by the longest way.

"He thinks he'll see if there was a man with me on the bus," said Mrs. Williams, who had also observed this procedure. I protested that the most devoted husband could hardly suppose she would be embarking on a liaison at the moment, but she said that the Welsh did not proceed by reasoning common to ordinary people.

About this time she began to try to talk me into getting an electric sewing-machine. She had a treadle one of her own, which it was always her pride and pleasure to lend me. She used to insist on dragging it round to our wing herself, and threading the shuttles ready for me. Now she began to lecture me on the fact that a good sewing-machine, to a woman tied to the house by children, represented independence. It meant that if you were down and out there was no need to make the choice between their going hungry or being left to set themselves on fire at home. Her sewing-machine had been her salvation when she could not leave Dick, as a baby, and her first husband was earning nothing. It was the one possession she had always refused to sell.

In the end I found myself, to my own surprise, giving way. She seemed so inexplicably satisfied, once she saw me using it, that I wondered if she wanted to use it herself. But she said off-handedly that she never fancied electricity.

One day I found her in the study, putting some books we had lent Dick back in the shelves, upside-down. She started when I came in.

"I brought these back," she said. "I know what a store you set by your books."

All the same, I never guessed. One evening I put my hand in the baby's bath-water and found it cold. I boiled a kettle and washed his face and hands and went downstairs to the study to work. I thought that perhaps Mrs. Williams had been cleaning the flues. They never forgot the boiler.

Later in the evening I suddenly looked up and found Williams before me. He said hoarsely:

"Where's my wife?"

I stared. He looked so odd. But he never got drunk. I said wonderingly that I supposed she was somewhere around their flat.

"She's gone off with Dick and left us," he said at last. He looked so stunned that I pulled him into a chair. He sat speechless. I fetched a mug of cider. He looked at it stupidly and then began to drink it. Half-way through he put it down and said fiercely:

"Did she tell you where she was going?"

"I didn't even know she'd gone."

I tried to realize it. When you have been supposing that someone is close to you, all day, and then find that she had been miles away all the time, you feel as if you had stepped on a stair that isn't there. For a year and a half she had been my constant companion, and closer to me than any of my own personal friends. In the mornings, when we met, we had known at the first glance how things were with each other. I remembered how we had discovered that "Queen Victoria's Promise" had been the first poem either of us had ever learned by heart, and how we used to recite it, prompting each other's memory, over the dishes. It was some minutes before I could even believe that all that was over.

"Has she taken her sewing-machine—the one I used to borrow?"

"It's not in the kitchen," he admitted.

Then I knew she had gone for good. I could have wept for the stricken giant, clutching his empty mug. At last he heaved himself out of the chair.

"You'll be needing hot water," he said. "I'll go and light the boiler."

I was alone that night, with the children. Long after I was asleep, it seemed, I was awakened by the telephone-bell. The voice of Mrs. Williams came over the line, distorted, a long way away.

"I had to speak to you," she said. "I want to thank you for everything and to tell you how sorry I am. But I had to do it."

"Yes, I know," I said.

"I'm not going to tell you where I am," said the far-away voice. "You've got to be able to tell him that you don't know. I don't want him to start setting on you."

"Can't you send him a message?"

"No," she said. The pips sounded.

"Please send a message for Jenny," I begged desperately.

"Tell her to be a good girl, and my love."

"Do you want another three minutes?" asked the operator. The telephone clicked and there was silence.

In the morning there was a tap at our door. Jenny came in. "It's very quiet in our flat," she said, in a thin little voice. "I wondered if you'd mind if I sat in here till school-time."

She sat down to share the other children's breakfast, but the tears rolled down on to her untouched plate. When the others went to get their coats, I gave her the message from her stepmother. I never wish to see such stunned grief on a child's face again.

"My hair," she whispered, as the others came in to tell her it was time for the school bus. Her father had plaited it for her, and the result was much what you would expect of a heavy engineer asked to turn his hand to hairdressing. I replaited it and she straightened her shoulders and went out to the bus.

Every evening after work, Williams went off to look for his wife. One night he came into the garden looking mysterious and triumphant. “I’m on her track,” he said. “I know where she is *and* who’s she with.”

He would not say any more. We hoped desperately that he would not find her. We wondered whether he would murder all three when he found them, or content himself with the mysterious third party in the drama.

A few nights later, the telephone rang. A masculine voice asked if Mrs. Williams was there. “Who are you, anyway?” I asked cautiously.

It was the police. Mrs. Williams and Dick had disappeared.

“Who reported it?” I managed to ask at last.

The police answered readily that it was the authorities at the Naval Hospital. They had been asked to send the ambulance to a different address recently and had picked Dick up there. The surgeons had decided to cut off Dick’s leg. He had appeared to take the prospect calmly, but when the ambulance reached his lodgings, he had vanished without trace. They were in a terrible fright in case he had come to the conclusion that he might as well make away with himself.

I told them then about the elopement and that possibly the three had simply found out that Williams was on their track. The police cheered up enormously. I added that I hoped no one would take any steps towards uniting the severed couple or anything like that.

“We don’t find people’s wives for them,” said the police curtly. “We haven’t got that much time to spare.”

Williams decided to move into the two-roomed cottage of his mother-in-law, the layer-out. Odd as the arrangement seemed, I was glad of it for Jenny’s sake. She had always referred to the old woman as her grannie and I had an idea that the layer-out herself had never really got it straight which were her grandchildren and which were not. I wrote to Jenny sometimes, and met her in the town, but any communication between us always consisted of her asking me, over and over again, if I had heard anything about her mum yet.

Williams borrowed the van which he had used to move in. He carried the wardrobe out of the manor on his back, and trundled the ancient piano, single-handed, and hauled it aboard. The new furniture went back to the hire-purchase firm. When he came to the bathroom and I was about to take down the curtains while he rolled up the matching lino, he stopped.

"I'd sooner leave it as it is," he said. He took a last look at his creation and went away.

A long time afterwards, I had been in London for the day and had settled myself in an empty carriage at Charing Cross. Just as the train was moving, a porter swung himself in and sat down opposite to me. Whenever I looked up, he was staring. At last he asked me if I had ever known anyone called Mrs. Williams.

"I thought it must be you," he said. "She talks about you, and she's got some snaps taken in that garden of yours, when Dick was alive."

He talked of her all the way until I got off at Ashford. His eyes twinkled as he described the things she said, and her comical way when she got herself into difficulties. He had been given a large tip that day, by a harassed traveller, and had slipped out of the station to a shop which had some sweets which she particularly fancied. He produced the box to show me and described—at great length—the series of *jeux-d'esprit* he proposed to use when presenting them to her. If I closed my eyes, I could imagine that I was sitting opposite to a boy of eighteen, talking of his first love. When I opened them, I saw a shabby, elderly porter from Charing Cross on his way home to Mrs. Williams. Was she so plain? The snapshot in my album of the manor says so. I don't know.

13

THE summer after the Williams went was moist and warm. Every morning, when we looked out of the window, it seemed as if the undergrowth had crept a few inches nearer to the house, during the night. There was no colour in the garden. Instead, a web of misty green seemed to be woven over it, as though it was the beginning of the hundred years of the Sleeping Beauty. There was no Williams to scythe and mow, no Mrs. Williams to weed and clip edges. We were sure that the three of us could manage it, with part-time help from Morris, if we devoted the whole of our spare time to the garden. We still feel that we could have done, if we had not somehow got three weeks behind. We could not say how, or when, but the garden had got a flying start on us, and we were always toiling in its wake, trying to catch up. The currants were over-ripe and sticky the day they were gathered. Nettles had started seeding before we cut them down. 'We had to tear away convolvulus before we could gather gooseberries. The motor-mower seized up on being asked to cut grass that was already almost scything-height.

"This won't do," said Bob. "Three amateurs can't defeat a jungle which used to take two full-time professional gardeners to keep it at bay. We don't want to be like the Russians, who didn't discover the wheel until everyone else had forgotten they ever had an Industrial Revolution."

He started our Industrial Revolution the very next Saturday. From now on, he said, the manor was going to be run by machinery. Six years ago, when we first arrived, I should have thought it Philistine. But now I had had enough human interest to last me a lifetime. If Bob had produced a staff of robots, I should have accepted them with a sigh of relief.

Instead of cutting nettles with scythes and bill-hooks, we got the farmer to come in with his hay-cutter and trundle it round orchards and lawns. We hired two men with a machine like a giant's electric razor for the hedges. In one afternoon they shaved the hedge which used to take Howard three weeks. For the vegetable-garden, we hired a firm with a motor-cultivator. Bob's invention stopped short of picking the fruit by machinery. Instead, we hired an entire troop of Boy Scouts, who swarmed up the trees and stripped them in one day, with only reasonable wastage from wolf-cubs sportingly shying apples at each other.

Cutting the year's logs, ready for winter, was another problem. We used to coerce guests into it, as exercise, which was an understatement. But they soon discovered that at the end of an afternoon of sweating slavery they had cut enough to keep the fire going for about twenty minutes, and any warmth they achieved was only a by-product. Bob found a man who owned an electric saw and was willing to bring it out to the manor for the whole of one Saturday if we would provide personnel to feed it. That struck a sinister note, which was in time with the day. There is no sound so macabre as the voice of an electric saw. It wails and shrieks and moans so that the air is full of lamentations. But the fact that depressed us most was that, as we watched the man set up his machine, we observed that he had three fingers missing off one hand.

"You can't help it sometimes, however quick you try to be," he remarked stolidly, when he saw our eyes riveted on it.

The whirling saw cut through logs as though they had been new bread. Our part was to push each log under the saw. It looked terribly easy. If you glanced round, at the next helper in the line, when you wanted the next piece, your hand went off the block with the previous one.

Once, when I was up in the house, boiling strong tea for everyone's nerves, and meditating about adding aspirin, the hideous screams of the saw stopped. I stood with the kettle in my hand, waiting for stumbling footsteps. They came. Bob arrived, clutching his wrist and dripping blood everywhere. "But I got it away in time," he said triumphantly. By the end of the day we looked as if we had all just emerged from a third-degree session.

The garden looked surprisingly tidy and productive. When we worked out our bills for the machinery, they added up to far less than a gardener's wage. And yet the garden looked as neat as it had under Howard's rule. We had even, in the enthusiasm of our industrial revolution, put pieces of land under cultivation which had been derelict when we arrived.

We had installed another ex-army couple with a child in the Williams' flat. We realized that we could never hope to find workers on the Williams level again. And we asked of the young man and wife was that they should stoke the boiler, dig their own piece of garden and that the wife should pursue our newly-bought electric cleaners and polishers over the vast floors of the manor.

It was very quiet, nowadays, around the manor. Each family lived its own self-contained life and the garden was empty and deserted, for days at a stretch. But it looked impressive. When we passed other people's overgrown gardens, we wondered, patronizingly, why they had never thought of simply doing the whole thing by machinery, twice a season or so.

We should have remembered that the manor was built to be waited upon by human beings. While we kept beds clear and grass mown, all those bits which are neither cultivated nor wild—the patches that make up the peculiar charm of an English garden—were quietly going native.

The ground-elder was the first pointer. While we had been busy with our stream-lined methods, it had a quiet few months for infiltration. It crept cautiously round the corner on to the front lawn. Hugging the wall behind the herbaceous border it crept along the bed and strangled the row of sentinel tiger-lilies. We suddenly awoke to the fact that the whole of the front plot was now occupied territory.

Ground-elder is the nearest thing to Triffids, the mobile plant of the science shocker. When I was working on it alone, I used to spin round and glare nervously at the long strands I had uprooted, sure that, since I last looked, one of them had edged itself a few inches nearer the flower-bed again. No matter how much you combed the beds, you would find half a dozen shoots there two days later.

The silence and the patches of thick undergrowth brought all sorts of creatures up near to the house, which we had never even seen on the outskirts of the garden before. Snakes wriggled unconcernedly across the drive. Moles churned up the lawn. And one mild evening of St. Martin's Summer, I came into the hall and thought I saw a little green creature, sitting with its little green hands before it and staring at me. I looked again, and found it was true.

It was a lizard. It had evidently wakened out of its winter sleep and come to the conclusion that if the weather was as warm as this it must be summer again. I suppose, as the evening began to grow chilly, it drifted into the house, though there was not, in fact, much difference in the temperature now that we had the fire as seldom as we could.

I opened the front door again and invited it to return to bed. But it refused to budge. When I lit the study fire it edged nearer to the study. I went to bed and left it there. Next morning it was still sitting there dreamily. I took up the question of its returning to wherever it hibernated, but the morning was cool and it wouldn't consider going out of doors at all.

It was an embarrassing guest. It put me off work, whenever I looked up. Also I was afraid someone would step on it and squash it. Finally I crossly put some leaves in a cigarette-box on the desk and left the lid a little bit open. I had an idea that if it would once go off to sleep again, I would transfer the whole thing out of doors and lend it the box till next summer. But it sat in the box wide awake and unblinking.

It was exasperating, being saddled with a lizard. It didn't touch the leaves and by afternoon I felt morally obliged to go up to the children's room and look through their nature-books to find out what lizards ate. The nature-books specified, at some length, what charming little creatures they were, which I considered inaccurate, but gave no practical information. The encyclopedia said they ate flies. I discovered that the one time in your life when you really need a dead fly is the one time when all the shelves and window-ledges are absolutely bare of them. I wasted half the day in vain.

It was Friday and we had friends coming for the week-end.

I didn't hear their car, and they came straight through into the study and stood in the doorway with the blood draining out of their faces. I looked in the direction of their horrified stare. The lid of the cigarette-box was opening slowly and a little green hand on a skinny green arm was emerging. It took about half a gallon of cider to restore their nerves. As a matter of fact, I became rather attached to it. It was like having a pet dragon by my side. But shortly afterwards it died, and I buried it in the garden.

That summer, the squirrels had ventured down from the trees at the end of the garden, to the ones close to the house. I used to fetch the children to watch the far-sighted little creatures laying away a store of nuts against the winter when the trees would be bare. I had an idea it would be good for the children's characters, as well as their knowledge of nature, because all the National Savings posters were featuring squirrel pictures at the time with a caption pointing out the moral.

But the squirrels either did not subscribe to the thrift theory or else were in an unusually giddy frame of mind that year.

They spent the nutting season in chasing each other wildly up and down the beech-trees. At last, with a perceptible lack of enthusiasm, they did bury a few nuts. I was exasperated because, out of all the four acres, they picked on the exact spot where I had planted lily of the valley. The plants had cost four and sixpence each, and I had felt guilty about it at the time. But the manor garden had never had any lily of the valley, and I fancied myself with a bunch pinned romantically on to my coat whenever I went out.

After the mild autumn, we had some snow. The squirrel's got up from their winter sleep—presumably in order not to miss the fun. Nothing I ever learned about hibernating creatures matched up with their behaviour around the manor. The whole thing, I found, was much less systematic than I had been led to believe. I grumbled about it to the farmer, who said he constantly met snakes, who should have been invisible and asleep, wandering about his fields at ploughing-time. The squirrels behaved as if they had booked for a winter-sports season. They scurried about in the snow, whisking it into floating clouds with their tails, chased each other about, and took leaps from one snow-clad bough to another, like skiers showing off. I crouched at the window, with the children, assuring them that any moment now the squirrels would go unerringly to their secret hoard.

Sure enough, they decided eventually that it was time for a snack and sobered up and came down from the tree and started digging. First they tried the lawn. Then they tried the rose-bed. It was agony to watch them. I wanted to open the window and shout irritably that they had better look under the lily of the valley. But they went on grubbing about, without even getting warm, until dusk, and next day they tried again. Then they gave up and, I suppose, went back to bed. Next summer I didn't have so much as a single sprig of lily of the valley to show for the time and money I had spent.

Indoors, it was so quiet that the mice moved in. There must have been a complete city, carved out by their forbears, inside the fabric of the manor. Once, when I found a whole army of them in the larder, I took a flashlight and went round the walls, to find out how they all disappeared so quickly without queueing. There were holes in the ceilings, in the corner of the walls, in the rafters and in the floor. I stopped them all up and they re-opened them again.

Then two strange children appeared at the door, with two soaking kittens which they had taken out of the river. Nothing would convince them that we had not put them in. We were obliged to install the kittens in the barn and feed them with a dolls' feeding-bottle, and found ourselves in the position of owing them a permanent living. The Tom was a reincarnation of the Industrious Apprentice, but the Tabby no better than she should be. She bit the hand that fed her from the moment she had strength enough to give a good nip and ran away from home at an early age. The Tom cleared the house of mice and then officiously took over the duties of the dog, Doubtful, now a hardened absentee. It used to welcome the men at the door when they came home and sit adoringly at their feet all evening.

One Sunday morning, when we went to the barn for hay for the hens' nest-boxes, there was the Tabby with two newborn kittens. The children were enchanted, but we privately agreed that the right place for females of her kind was a cats' home. Next day she deserted them and Jane got out her dolls' feeding-bottles again. One kitten began to thrive. The other, which was a grey one and quite pretty, got weaker and weaker. We found Richard weeping heart-broken tears in a corner of the garden. None of the masters at his school had ever succeeded in disturbing his composure, with the best will in the world.

"It's too weak to lap," he kept on saying, over and over again, like Saul lamenting Jonathan.

Next morning, when I found it dead, I could not imagine how I was going to break the news to him. I wandered down by the river, thinking what to say. My foot struck a stone in the long grass and I picked it up mechanically and replaced it. Long ago, when we first came, we had discovered that this spot was an animals' burial-ground. There were miniature gravestones, some fallen, some at a drunken angle, like a neglected churchyard. They had names of horses and dogs on them, and dates, and tight-lipped comments, like "A Faithful Friend". Now it struck me that what had consoled the Colonel might also console Richard. I found him face downwards, in frozen grief. "Get up and pick some flowers," I said. "We've got a funeral to arrange."

Sure enough, by the time we had buried the kitten and put up a stone, Richard was perfectly calm again. He spent some time arranging flowers and cutting the grass, and from then on attached himself to the surviving kitten. The last thing we wanted was an extra cat, but we had no choice. It used to crawl into Richard's bed at night. I was pretty sure it had fleas. So I took to putting its meals at the barn door, hoping it would decide to live in the stables. But the only result was that cats from miles around used to come and sit about, waiting for the plate to be filled. Once I took a census of cats living off the manor. There were fifteen, including three that belonged to Morris's wife. When I visualized the future, if they were all going to decide that there were cat-lovers in residence, and deposit their little bundles in the barn, I couldn't see what was to become of us. We had the sense of living in the decline of a civilization. Week by week, the jungle moved a step nearer to the house. The vegetable garden was full of scutterings, as moor-hens raced back from the pea-bed to the river Once, a bag of sugar burst in my locked store-room and dripped on to the stone floor. Some far-flung ant scout discovered it, and I found an immense army of ants, in disciplined formation, streaming right in from the garden, down the passage and under the door. The high shelf we kept for dangerous drugs began to look like an arsenal for chemical warfare, with weed-killer, ant-killer, wasp-killer, mouse-poison and mole-traps.

Then the pestilence struck.

All of a sudden, we were front-page news. The rumour was that one of the farmers had realized he had a case of foot-and-mouth among his stock, but had kept it dark. If you reported it, your stock was slaughtered. It spread. Farm after farm was hit. We were forbidden to cross fields. No animal of any kind could move from one place to another. If dogs were seen loose, they were shot.

We shut up the dog Doubtful in the dog-house, from which he filled the garden with lamentations. The clientele for my cats' canteen dwindled unaccountably. There were days when I should have been glad to see one of the old faces again. Perhaps they were shot. Morris's wife, for the first time since I had known her, suddenly turned animated and passionate and told me that she had heard for certain that the government was secretly putting down cat-poison. She kept her three indoors.

Kent was desolated. From the road, there was no sign of life on any farm. No one was moving about the yard; no one loading fodder on to a cart; no living creature of any kind in the fields. But above all, the silence struck chill. We had never realized that we lived in a constant background of bleating and mooing and neighing until now, when only the howling of uneasy, imprisoned dogs could be heard. The saddest time was early evening, when there should have been the bustle of milking around the farmyard. You would see the farmer and his wife standing motionless in front of their house, apparently at a complete loss as to how one spent this hour of the day if there were no animals to see to.

Over and over again, we counted the days of quarantine, and each time, just as we neared the end, a new farm developed the infection. We achieved the gloomy distinction of being the hardest hit village in the country. All the national papers began to print—"Seven Days More for Worst Hit Village", then, six, five and so on. But we never reached release.

Along the river, the farmer emptied his sheds of the useless fodder for his stock. Soon afterwards, I began to think I saw grey shapes in the dusk, gliding among the nettles. I wondered if some of the outlawed cats were lurking about, wild and hungry.

The old labourer, who was Mollie's father-in-law, used to scythe grass the other side of the river. He was surly and we never exchanged a good-day. When I went down with the bucket of hens' food, he always knocked off work and took up a spectator stance. One day he called out:

"Hey!"

"What?"

"There's rats after you." I hastily drew away from the long grass and went down to the river's edge.

"How do you mean?"

"I been watching you all week," he said. "When you goes back to the house, there's a line of them comes out of the river and over the wall and eats your hens' stuff."

I felt exactly the same sick fright I had when I was eighteen and found a greasy, middle-aged man was following me through Brussels. I thought I had thrown him off and then, as I was trying on a hat, saw his face close behind mine in the mirror.

I put the hens' mash in their feeding-bowls and went away across the stableyard and climbed on a wall and waited. After a moment I saw a dark shape slide up over the henyard wall and drop over, then another and another. There was an indignant squawking among the hens and they went fluttering about the yard. In a panic between fury and fear I dashed over and flung the empty bucket over the wall at the rats. The hens went into hysterics. The rats quietly glided away over the wall and back into the river. Mr. Harris watched with spiteful appreciation.

"That won't do no good," he said with satisfaction.

"All right. You make a better suggestion," I shouted crossly. But he went back to his work, much refreshed by the entertainment.

One thing was clear. I could not face that henyard again in the evening, watching the clumps of nettles for a faint movement among their stalks. I had to move all the hens into the barn. You are supposed to move hens after dark. For one thing, it is easier, because you just unhook them from their roosts and carry them head downwards, holding them by the feet, which method of transport they are said to prefer to any other, though I always find it difficult to believe. The other reason is that being moved after dark is said to upset them less psychologically than being asked to accept new quarters by daylight. However, mine had to take a chance on getting complexes this time and I lured and chased them into the barn and locked the door.

The hens openly detested living in the barn. They spent all day trying to get out. If we let them, they went back to their old roost, in the henyard, at dusk, which meant going in there, with teeth set and slacks tucked into one's socks, to collect them and take them to safety. If we kept them locked in, they pined and moped, and laid no eggs. In any case, if they did lay them, we had to search for them through the hay. Then there began to be rustlings in the hay and we found an egg which had been rolled across the floor to a newly-made hole in the wooden side of the barn.

We began to understand why one regards moles with detachment, squirrels with sentimental fondness, rabbits with resigned amusement, mice with disgusted impatience, but rats with fear and horror. It is because you have the sense of a mind working against you. Morris told us that there was almost certainly one old rat, leading the gang, who had lived long enough to know all the answers. He said you could tell a gang leader by his size, and that there was one he had seen which was unusually large. We moved the hens again, into the stable, and found that the rats were swarming up to the hay-loft and getting down the open trap for lowering hay into the boxes.

Morris got out the old traps from Howard's shed and laid them, but we never caught any. The brains of the outfit had probably seen and been warned about them by his grandad long ago. We got obsessed by the idea of outwitting him.

When I was shopping in Ashford, I found Geronwy with a stall in the market-place. The weekly market was pitiful, now that there were no cows and sheep for miles around, and that the few left were under house arrest in their own farms. There were rows and rows of empty pens; a few hens and ducks, and the stalls where farmers' wives could buy ribbon and tape and nylons and the men Wellington boots and mackintoshes. The farmers were coming in to hang about and look at milking-stools just for something to do. Geronwy was selling them guns and cartridges, now that they had time to go shooting. I told Geronwy about the rats and he said he would come out to the manor and shoot them.

"With a muzzle-loader?" I asked nervously.

He said coldly that you did not use a muzzle-loader on vermin like rats. He turned up with two or three rifles, several boxes of cartridges and a ground-sheet in jagged patches of green and dun for camouflage.

We laid an ambush. We locked all the hens up, out of the reach of stray bullets. Geronwy took up a post lying in the bushes near the river's edge. As the church clock struck five, which was the hens' feeding-time, I came out of the house as usual, with my bucket of mash. Walking into the henyard with Geronwy's rifle trained on me made me feel exactly like the heroine of a Resistance play on television, which was the staple diet of our entertainment at the time. I poured the swill into the trough and walked away—trying to go no faster than usual. Then I climbed on the wall to watch. After a few moments' pause, the rats came slinking over the wall, in the usual long fast-moving line. Geronwy waited till the last one had reached the trough, then he fired. It was wonderful, seeing the flashes, hearing the repeated crack of the rifle and knowing that one's hidden enemies were out in the open at last, being attacked. Geronwy picked off five before the last one reached the safety of the river.

After that, they laid low for a week. But we knew, from the size of the corpses that we had not got the leader of the gang yet. All they did was to avoid the times I might be expected to be around. Once or twice, when I went down to the river to peg clothes out, I heard a hysterical squawking in the yard, and saw one or two hens ruffling up their feathers and jumping up to peck at something sitting in a crevice of the wall. I was ashamed of myself that I didn't go in and take their part, considering that they were pitting their beaks against rats' teeth and their hen-witted brains against the cunning which was baffling us. Instead I rang up the Council and was impressed by being put through to the Rodent Operator's office. He came round next day. As soon as I opened the door he said at once:

"You've been putting poison down."

I denied it.

"You'd better tell me, you know," he said patiently. "I know how it is. Ladies always use poison, and they mostly say they haven't."

I begged him to believe that my conscience was absolutely clear and asked him why he minded so much.

"When ladies put down poison—and it's not often I meet one like you who doesn't—the rats won't eat *my* poison and there's nothing I can do."

I confessed to the trap.

"Did you catch any?"

"Not one."

"That's all right then," he said. "You don't want to get them nervous."

I confessed to the gun.

"Did it seem to upset them at all?"

"They took it in their stride."

He considered and said that if I was sure I had not put them on their guard in any other way, he thought he would be able to do something for me. He had a series of little wooden boxes, with narrow entrances and exits. A hen could not even get its beak in, but a rat could just squeeze itself through. I wondered why he made the poison so difficult to achieve.

"You have to, with rats," he explained. "If they find it's easy to get, they think you're up to something. You got to make them think they shouldn't be there to make them feel easy."

Next week he came and took all the little boxes away, saying that the poison had gone.

We could not believe it at first. We still found ourselves making wide detours round clumps of nettles, avoiding long grass and not going into any of the sheds after dusk. We still looked nervously over our shoulders at the slightest rustle. After a time, we got more confidence. We cleaned out the henyards, put the hens back in them and recognized stray cats at dusk (when all cats are grey) merely as stray cats.

The dog Doubtful, maddened by confinement, found that he could scramble up the fencing gate of the dog-house, escaped, went tearing out of the gate and was killed by a car, which was not expecting loose dogs to appear on Kent's deserted roads.

Now there was complete and utter silence on the manor. There were no sheep lowing in the field; no cows at the end of the paddock and no dog to raise his voice at the sound of footsteps. We had not been able to buy new pigs this season, since the market was closed, so the very pig-sty was silent and deserted. The grass grew waist-high by the river;

the nettles flourished; the ground-elder choked the flowers. I was expecting a baby and the amount of physical labour I could put in was strictly limited by the doctor. It was like keeping house in a devastated area. Every day the desolation and neglect seemed to thicken, over the fields and the house and garden.

Then came the day that finished me with the manor for ever. I look at her now, if I pass her roofs and clustering trees and river running through the garden, on the way to Dover, with only a detached dislike. It is like looking at someone you once loved and then hated and now merely wish to forget.

It started with the water-supply failing. I turned on the taps in the morning and got a hollow whistle. I was alone in the house except for the baby. I got my buckets and went to the river. On my way back I went to cut a lettuce for lunch and found they were all seeding. I pulled up an armful for the hens and went down to the yard with them. While the hens gleefully squabbled over them, I idly went into the hen-house to collect eggs. As I put my hand in the nesting-box something glided over my hand and up my bare arm and went quietly away over the floor. It slipped into a hole in the opposite wall and near to the hole I saw there was a dead hen.

By the time I got back to the house, shivering and pouring with sweat, it occurred to me that I ought not to leave the corpse there, in case it brought more rats. Everyone was out. I hung about, making a long business of selecting a garden fork and putting on Wellingtons and thick gloves, and finally opened the henyard gate with my heart in my mouth.

In the shadowy hen-house, a whole pack of rats looked up at me, from a sit-down meal of the corpse and made no attempt to move. I remembered that when they get into a bold enough frame of mind, they will run up the handle of your implement and get at you. I threw the fork at them and bolted to the gate. But I had to get that horrible eyeless skeleton underground and I went back and found the rats gone, and dragged it away up the garden where I threw a few spadesful of earth over it until Morris should come back at tea-time.

The next forty-eight hours was a misty, but (in fact) not disagreeable period of time in which I lay in the Magnolia Room watching it alternately disappear from view and assemble itself again, punctuated by finding people—apparently materialized out of thin air, like genii—standing beside me with cups of tea or glasses of brandy. It was my first experience of drifting close to death, and I may say that it is pleasant to know (for future reference) that it is neither terrifying nor particularly upsetting. It is, for instance, nothing like as bad as being really sea-sick. It is rather like looking out of the window as you sit in a train. What goes on, from your dreamy vantage-point, is interesting, but does not concern you to any great extent. Even when some ambulance-men turned up with a stretcher, and I found myself driving along the lane where I usually cycled, it was not surprising. At the hospital they told me there would be no baby, either now or at any other time. It seemed as if I had always known. I only thought that now perhaps the manor would be satisfied. Since we got into her clutches, eight years ago, she had been an insatiable mistress, demanding every penny, every ounce of energy, every hour of our tune and now she had sucked me dry. Now there was nothing more she could take and I was finished with her, glad to get away—but only just, so they told me—with my life.

I discovered a useful fact about hospital. The endearments used by the staff are in direct ratio to your condition. The first night I was brought in I was the night-nurse's "little sweetheart"; the next day "darling", but the following one only "dear". The morning that the day-sister greeted me with "Smoking away like an old chimney as usual, Mrs. Adam?"

I was not surprised to learn that I might go home right away.

Back in the Magnolia Room, I savoured the silence. Outside, the wistaria was launched on its second flowering of the year. The blossom hung in clusters of faint silvery purple, like grapes in a fairy-tale.

At dusk, two swallows came in from the garden. As long as I left the light on, they flew in measured circles, round and round the ceiling, gleaming blue-black against the white. When I put out the light, the faint rushing of their wings ceased. When I woke, with the dawn, they were circling round again. I was sure that they were the swallows for whose sake I left the stable-door open, all summer, so that they could go in and out to their nest in the corner above the manger. I watched them, as the light strengthened, until they flew away through the window. I went down to the stable that day, but it was empty and deserted. I knew then that I should never see them again. By the time they came back in the spring, we should be gone.

14

WE FOUND a flat in London and agreed to show prospective tenants over the manor at all reasonable times.

The house-agents dug through their files and found the advertisement which had lured us to disaster. They put it in the Personal column of *The Times*.

From the day it appeared, the telephone began to ring at all times, reasonable and unreasonable. I developed a mechanical patter, like the Beefeaters in the Tower.

"This is the old dining-hall," I said. "The carvings represent the four evangelists. That wooden one above the fireplace, with a wooden ribbon bow on top is so valuable that it is insured separately. There are two secret drawers in the Sheraton cabinet. This is how you open them. As you see, we keep our National Health cards inside. This is the drawing-room. The Dutch tiles are each a collector's piece, but unfortunately when they installed the Adams fireplace they stuck it over the top row so that only half of each picture is visible. Those rows of legs at the top right represent the armies walking round the walls of Jericho."

"Beautiful," they murmured. As a matter of fact they were hideous.

"This is the dressing-room which belongs to what used to be the Colonel's bedroom."

"I've been thinking," said one of the wives brightly. "Couldn't this little dressing-room be turned into a bathroom?" I felt the reproachful ghost of Howard at my elbow. I paid no attention to it. If he had not dismissed the Brigadier's wife, on this very question, she would have had the manor instead of us, and we should have been solvent now, with comfortable bank-balances. Also, we should have had another child, instead of a confused memory of near-disaster and a hidden disappointment that was never going to be wiped out.

"A very good idea," I answered glibly. "I should insist on it if I were you."

"This is the main kitchen, the servants' hall, the butler's pantry, the butler's bedroom, the game-larder, the new bathroom and this is the boot-room."

"What do you use it for?"

"For cleaning boots. The woodshed here is for kindling; the one near the stables for cut wood; and the one near the river for wood waiting to be cut. The one next to that is used by the farmer, whose roof you see across the fields, for storing his spare machinery."

"Who does the motor-cycle belong to?" asked one of the husbands, who had been snooping in the shed beyond.

"That I don't know," I said. "Now you mention it, I've seen a man coming up and down the right-of-way with a motor-cycle. When the war was still on, I thought he must be in the Home Guard, but that was eight years ago. Next time I happen to be about when he passes, I'll make a point of asking him."

They all stood about, staring at the copper-beech glowing against the green, and at the lawns rolling away to the fields beyond, and the river slipping by and the wild orchids at the foot of the old tree and the squirrels chasing each other up and down. They looked neither approving nor disapproving, but simply dazed.

"Have you had any nibbles yet?" I asked the house-agents every day.

"Not yet," they would say. "But we've got another good batch coming down tomorrow."

But one Saturday afternoon a car piled high with children and dogs drove in at the gate and the owners of it asked apologetically if they were too late. They were artists.

They instantly fell in love with the manor. They said they had always planned to have just such a house, with wistaria over the windows and a river running through the garden. We took to them at first sight and it made us uneasy to hear them talk like that.

"It's got thirty-three rooms, you know," we reminded them gloomily.

"We could get some friends to share it with us."

"It's awfully difficult to get enough service to keep it going."

"We could get a strong married couple to live in the kitchen wing."

"And there's four acres of garden."

"Do it seasonally, by machinery," said the husband briskly.

*

The house-agent made a strange remark as we came to the last of our business of letting the manor as a combined effort.

"I *have* enjoyed our acquaintance," he said wistfully. "I'm quite sorry to think it's over."

"Then come and call on us in London," we consoled him.

He shook his head and looked brooding. He walked off, then came back.

"I say," he said. "We've got so friendly, you know. I say, you won't feel too hardly towards me, will you? I mean, you'll know I've got my living to earn. These things are part of our business."

"Yes, of course," we said, utterly perplexed. He spoke as heavily as if we should be cursing his name in three months' time. Sure enough, we were.

We had three months in which to clear the house. We started in the attics and worked down. Digging through from strata to strata of stored goods was like archaeology, with the most recent period on top. First came Post-Utility; then Utility; below that the restricted period of clothing coupons which came before it, when every piece of rag had a value and one never threw anything away. Below that was all the stuff our friends had dumped on us, because we had so much storage-space that we should never notice.

But below that was a strata of possessions belonging to the Colonel and the Colonel's parents, who had also never thrown anything away. Once I came upon a damask crinoline skirt, folded carefully among the seed-boxes in the potting-shed. It fell to pieces as I lifted it down, and floated about the dusky shed and the fragments drifted out of the door, like the ghost of the lady of long ago who had worn it and unaccountably left it there.

In the locked paraffin-shed was a set of eight locked iron safes, with the Colonel's name on them. Any locked safe is irresistible.

"Let's try Howard's bunch of keys," we said.

We had tried them so often that we thought we knew all their possibilities now. However, one of the children was sent indoors and came back rattling them.

"It might be the eight little ones which were always too small for anything else," said Colin. It was. The locks turned readily.

Inside there was the diary of an old parson who had lived in the manor, back in the eighteen-seventies. We sat down on the barrels of paraffin to study it. It was mostly accounts. Every year he had out-run his income by a little more. There were a lot of answers to begging letters he had written to his relatives, because he ran into debt. They were intolerably moral.

"Do you know what?" said my husband, studying the figures. "This reminds me disturbingly of our Bank Statements."

"At least the manor hasn't succeeded into running us into debt," I said consolingly. We had come into it with some money, and were going out penniless, but able, like the village blacksmith, to look the whole world in the face for we owed not any man.

By the time we had finished clearing the outhouses, the relics dated to the beginning of the century and we realized that this was its first complete spring-clean within living memory.

We lit a bonfire down by the river. For one whole month it burned steadily, day and night. In the mornings, it would still be smouldering, trying to devour the last bits of yesterday's rubbish, and when we added the first pile of the morning, it would start shooting up towards the sky again.

We separated one quarter of our furniture from the rest. In future we were going to live in less than one quarter of the space. When we looked at the three-quarters that were left, there seemed to be an awful lot of it.

We consulted the local auctioneer.

"Not the class of thing for our sales at all," he said. "Try some of those little second-hand shops where they sell all sorts."

"No use to us," said the junk-men. "Couldn't get a penny for it."

It is always wounding, when traders despise the things you have been using every day. They know this, and rely upon it to break your spirit.

"How about this?" I asked one of them, showing him a wooden bench we used in the hall when we needed extra seats.

"No good at all," said the junk-man.

"But it's an antique. Good-class stuff. It's a bargain at five guineas."

"That worm-eaten bit of deal?"

"Well, that's what you said when you sold it to us, anyway."

"You haven't looked after it properly," he said.

"I don't mind taking a few of the best things away if you just want them moved," said one of the men at last. "It wouldn't be worth my while to pay you anything, but then again I shan't ask you any money for the transport. But that's the best I can do."

It was enough. The worms turned. We held a consultation and came back to them.

"You can all go home again," we said offensively. "We've got an idea."

From every corner of the house, from attic and cellar and outhouse, we collected everything that had been just too good to burn. We put all outdoor equipment in the barn and all indoor goods into the old dining-room, whence they overflowed into the hall and right on to the front doorstep. Our price fixing was simple. Everything near the door was half-a-crown; everything next to that five shillings and so on. One or two prize objects, such as an air-fanned paraffin stove, the baby's outgrown cot and the piano were in the study, where we planned to entertain moneyed clients. Then we put an advertisement in the local paper and waited.

The *Kentish Express* comes out on Fridays. On Friday morning, as we were having breakfast, the bus stopped at our gate and disgorged a stream like a factory outing. They all hurried breathlessly up the drive. They calmed down a little when they saw the rooms.

Selling up the old home was one of the classical tragic scenes in Victorian novels. This was sheer, unadulterated pleasure. All the junk over which we had laboured began to be tidied away, as if it had taken wings, and each time a bit disappeared, coins clanked into the empty jam-jar on the mantelpiece. It was one person's job to keep on emptying it. We snatched our meals in brief intervals, interrupted every two minutes by the glad cry of "Sho-o-op!" from the one left on duty, finding he could not stem the tide of customers single-handed. We also had a warm feeling of philanthropy. We were making everyone so very happy. All the village wives and mothers spent hours rummaging among the piles, like children in a fairy-tale bran-tub which never runs dry.

From this immensely successful experiment I have learned what I shall do if I ever set up shop for a living. I shall concentrate on flower-pots, of all shapes, sizes and conditions. The barn, where the husbands did their purchasing, was cleared before anywhere else and it was pitiful to see the disappointment of those who had been unable to get there until the midday break, and found the last flower-pot gone. The stock I shall avoid is pianos. No one gave ours a second glance, even when its price had been reduced to nothing at all.

During the afternoon, I noticed a familiar hand-barrow parked outside the front door. Across the crowded room, I recognized the face of my old enemy, the lowest and least of the junk-shopkeepers. I remembered the number of times he had refused to reach me down something I wanted from the back of the shop. I thought of the times he had outbid me over old wooden chairs and bamboo tables at the local auctions. I pretended not to see him, but he followed me round.

"Those little red boots," he said, in the hateful hoarse voice that had so often capped my "Five shillings," with "Seven and a tanner." "They're about the size of my youngest kid."

"Oh yes?" I said uninterestedly.

"You got them among the Two-bob lot."

"A mistake," I said. "They should be in the half-crown section."

I moved them over and went on. He followed me.

"Course, they're very worn at the heels."

"I'm glad you don't want them," I said absently. "I promised I'd keep them for a lady from Appledore."

When I had served a neighbouring farmer's wife with a suit which had first belonged to my rich aunt and then to my sisters and myself in turns and was now back in fashion, I found him at my elbow again.

"I could give you four bob for the red ones and them little blue ones to match."

"Sorry," I said. "That gentleman there brought them back from Egypt as a present for the children, which gives them a high sentimental value barely covered by five shillings."

He pulled the money out of his pocket. It was interesting to discover what really touched the heart of a junk-man, accustomed to deal carelessly with such charming things as old lockets, Victorian annuals and wooden writing-boxes lined with faded velvet. But the shoes, which Bob had bought in Cairo long ago, and shipped home in his kit were, as a matter-of-fact, straight out of a fairy-tale, with turned-up toes and bead embroidery.

But when we collected the shoes from the heap there was only one blue one. His dismay would have softened any heart but mine. But I had eight years of resentment to work off.

"I'll tell you what I'll do for you," I said. "I shall probably be tidying this place out next Friday, or the Friday after. You can come back then if you want to."

But after he had gone away, sadly pushing his barrow, I knelt down and dragged the little blue shoe from under the bookcase, and told Jane to run after him with it.

We counted the money and it came to seventy pounds. "And we nearly paid someone to take it away," we reflected.

The floor was strewn with the final rejects, which included a man's dress-suit, curtains, bed-covers, jerseys, an old basket armchair and a washstand. We thought of the rag-and-bone man in the village, who was for ever coming round to the back door with his sack and offering money for bits of old rag. We decided to give him all the remains of the sale, free of charge.

"He won't have to work again for years," we said to each other benevolently.

He came in looking surly, but we put it down to being stunned by this unexpected piece of luck. We left him alone with the pile to savour his windfall. When we came back, he was still standing there with his old sack on his shoulder.

"What you going to pay me?" he asked.

"You mean, what do we want you to pay? Nothing. It's all for you. A parting gift."

"I mean what I say. What you going to pay for taking the stuff away? You don't think I'm going to move it all for you free?"

"But you collect rags for a living. You can collect all these at once."

"Not without you pay me to take them. There's the transport to think of."

"But you've got that barrow of yours, that you always push around, outside the door."

"That's right. What you going to pay me for bringing it down to take this stuff away?"

When he at last got it over, we were speechless with rage. We were exhausted with the sale, and dirty and dusty from clearing out the house and our fingers could not forget the rough, grimy, sticky feeling of old things that have been laid away too long. We grabbed every single thing that was left and took it down to the bonfire. Last of all, we piled the wash-stand and the basket armchair on to the top of the heap. A tall thin flame shot up higher than the barn roof and then, with a rush and a roar the blaze came into its own. It was magnificent. I learned afterwards that they had leaned out of their upper windows, all over the village, telling each other that we had set fire to the manor before we left it.

It was the last night. The men with the motor-plough and the men with the giant's electric razor and the farmer with his hay-cutter had trimmed the garden. Mollie and Noel had come down from the village and scrubbed the house from end to end. The hens were sold and the rats (we hoped) starving to death without them. Our packing was done and the picked quarter of furniture ready for the removal van. Every corner and every closet was cleared. Our footsteps echoed in the empty rooms.

"The piano!" we said, staring incredulously at it. There it stood, where it always had, in its place in the old dining-hall. We had already begged the artist and his wife to accept it as a parting gift, and they had refused with some firmness. They had a grand piano of their own and did not think they would require a second. We had offered it to every boys' club in Kent and had it accepted gratefully—provided we would transport it to the club quarters. Transport estimates had never been under ten pounds.

"Would it burn?" one of us suggested.

"We should never get it started. In any case, we've cleaned up the space where the bonfire was."

It was midnight and we were moving next day. There was nothing for it but a little deception. We got out our brooms and mops and took their handles off to use as rollers, and dragged it out to the dark paraffin-shed. Even by day, no light penetrated into its corners. We pushed the piano into the most obscure one, and locked the door, feeling as if we were turning the key on a skeleton. We hung up the duffle-coats which we had used for every outside job all these years and which we were bequeathing—this time with the legatees' consent—to the artist and his wife. For the last time we went to bed up the stairway with its carved banister-posts and met the bat who swooped about the house nightly and was always proceeding in the reverse direction when I went down the passage to the bathroom. Next day was Ladyday and exactly eight years since we moved in.

On Ladyday the sun shone and small white clouds floated about the sky. The removal-men kept on staring at the daffodils as though they thought they were seeing double. They seemed to take a terribly long time to get the vans loaded. All the time I was afraid that something was going to happen to stop us getting out of the manor. I longed for it to be empty and to be safely on the train. I couldn't believe that, after eight years' servitude, we were going to be allowed to escape. But next morning we awoke to the sound of lorries and workmen's buses. There was no desperate rush to catch the commuting train, no impatient creatures to feed, no freshly-grown weeds to uproot from the drive, no paraffin-stove to light, no logs to haul up from the shed. How did people who lived in London spend the freedom which they so carelessly took for granted?

It was a long time before we could really believe that we were free. We had a haunted feeling that the manor would not let us escape without a struggle. Liaisons are not to be disposed of so comfortably.

Night after night, I dreamed the same dream. I was standing outside the front door of the manor, guilty and anxious. Always I went in, through the familiar door, past the carved wolf and fox and down to the pegs where we had left our duffle-coats. The pockets, in real life, had always been full of an indescribable collection of objects—screws and wire-cutters, bits of string, garden scissors, keys and flashlights. In my dream, I always had to empty them. One morning, when the dream-pilgrimage had been more than usually unhappy, I was driven to telephoning the manor and telling the artist's wife that we had forgotten to empty the pockets before we left, and that I was tired of expiating my carelessness, night after night. I also confessed to the piano hidden in the paraffin-shed, in case my sub-conscious should have got mixed up among the various bits of guilt. She was very understanding—took the piano in her stride and undertook to empty the pockets as soon as she put down the telephone. I hoped that now I had shaken the manor's clutch from off my shoulder.

The postman deposited a fat packet on our mat. It was from the house-agent, who had been so friendly over re-letting the manor. It was a list of "dilapidations" twenty pages long, and ended by requesting a cheque for seven hundred and twenty pounds, at our convenience.

Only those who have been caught in a legal wrangle know how it poisons your whole life—how it turns up again just as you are beginning to forget it and be happy—how you learn to dread the post and look forward to Sunday when no letters come—how each letter is a little more disagreeable than the last and yet takes you no step nearer to a conclusion. We began to bore our friends because we could not talk of anything but our obsession. We could not think of anything else for long.

At last it was agreed that the debt should be settled within a certain time. We tore up prospectuses of the schools to which we had planned to send the children and entered the younger ones at the local primary school. We took on extra work and cut down our household expenses at every point. From seventy miles away, beyond the hop-fields and the white orchards of Kent, the manor stretched out her hand and kept us enslaved. Our time and money were not our own, any more than they had been over the last eight years.

The friends who used to come down and stay still remember her wistfully.

"Remember the lilacs and the roses? Remember bathing in the river? Remember the dawn chorus? Remember those swallows in the stable? Remember that cricket-match?"

We do not. Never again will we fall in love with a house. From now on, we mean to live in a series of impersonal flats, each one exactly like a hundred others in the block.

Even in April, when we buy daffodils off a street-barrow and say to each other, as we take them home, "I suppose the magnolia must be out," we always add, "Thank goodness, someone else has got to sweep up the fallen petals."

THE END

FURROWED MIDDLEBROW

FM1. *A Footman for the Peacock* (1940) . . . . RACHEL FERGUSON
FM2. *Evenfield* (1942) . . . . RACHEL FERGUSON
FM3. *A Harp in Lowndes Square* (1936) . . . . RACHEL FERGUSON
FM4. *A Chelsea Concerto* (1959) . . . . FRANCES FAVIELL
FM5. *The Dancing Bear* (1954) . . . . FRANCES FAVIELL
FM6. *A House on the Rhine* (1955) . . . . FRANCES FAVIELL
FM7. *Thalia* (1957) . . . . FRANCES FAVIELL
FM8. *The Fledgeling* (1958) . . . . FRANCES FAVIELL
FM9. *Bewildering Cares* (1940) . . . . WINIFRED PECK
FM10. *Tom Tiddler's Ground* (1941) . . . . URSULA ORANGE
FM11. *Begin Again* (1936) . . . . URSULA ORANGE
FM12. *Company in the Evening* (1944) . . . . URSULA ORANGE
FM13. *The Late Mrs. Prioleau* (1946) . . . . MONICA TINDALL
FM14. *Bramton Wick* (1952) . . . . ELIZABETH FAIR
FM15. *Landscape in Sunlight* (1953) . . . . ELIZABETH FAIR
FM16. *The Native Heath* (1954) . . . . ELIZABETH FAIR
FM17. *Seaview House* (1955) . . . . ELIZABETH FAIR
FM18. *A Winter Away* (1957) . . . . ELIZABETH FAIR
FM19. *The Mingham Air* (1960) . . . . ELIZABETH FAIR
FM20. *The Lark* (1922) . . . . E. NESBIT
FM21. *Smouldering Fire* (1935) . . . . D.E. STEVENSON
FM22. *Spring Magic* (1942) . . . . D.E. STEVENSON
FM23. *Mrs. Tim Carries On* (1941) . . . . D.E. STEVENSON
FM24. *Mrs. Tim Gets a Job* (1947) . . . . D.E. STEVENSON
FM25. *Mrs. Tim Flies Home* (1952) . . . . D.E. STEVENSON
FM26. *Alice* (1949) . . . . ELIZABETH ELIOT
FM27. *Henry* (1950) . . . . ELIZABETH ELIOT
FM28. *Mrs. Martell* (1953) . . . . ELIZABETH ELIOT
FM29. *Cecil* (1962) . . . . ELIZABETH ELIOT
FM30. *Nothing to Report* (1940) . . . . CAROLA OMAN
FM31. *Somewhere in England* (1943) . . . . CAROLA OMAN
FM32. *Spam Tomorrow* (1956) . . . . VERILY ANDERSON
FM33. *Peace, Perfect Peace* (1947) . . . . JOSEPHINE KAMM

FM34. *Beneath the Visiting Moon* (1940) . . . . ROMILLY CAVAN
FM35. *Table Two* (1942) . . . . MARJORIE WILENSKI
FM36. *The House Opposite* (1943) . . . . BARBARA NOBLE
FM37. *Miss Carter and the Ifrit* (1945) . . . . SUSAN ALICE KERBY
FM38. *Wine of Honour* (1945) . . . . BARBARA BEAUCHAMP
FM39. *A Game of Snakes and Ladders* (1938, 1955) . . . .
. . . . DORIS LANGLEY MOORE
FM40. *Not at Home* (1948) . . . . DORIS LANGLEY MOORE
FM41. *All Done by Kindness* (1951) . . . . DORIS LANGLEY MOORE
FM42. *My Caravaggio Style* (1959) . . . . DORIS LANGLEY MOORE
FM43. *Vittoria Cottage* (1949) . . . . D.E. STEVENSON
FM44. *Music in the Hills* (1950) . . . . D.E. STEVENSON
FM45. *Winter and Rough Weather* (1951) . . . . . . D.E. STEVENSON
FM46. *Fresh from the Country* (1960) . . . . MISS READ
FM47. *Miss Mole* (1930) . . . . E.H. YOUNG
FM48. *A House in the Country* (1957) . . . . RUTH ADAM
FM49. *Much Dithering* (1937) . . . . DOROTHY LAMBERT
FM50. *Miss Plum and Miss Penny* (1959) . DOROTHY EVELYN SMITH
FM51. *Village Story* (1951) . . . . CELIA BUCKMASTER
FM52. *Family Ties* (1952) . . . . CELIA BUCKMASTER

Printed in Great Britain
by Amazon

10242737R00119